Playing with Fire

T0283050

Amanda Kabak

Other Bella Books by Amanda Kabak

Training for Love

About the Author

Amanda Kabak is the author of the novels *Upended* and *The Mathematics of Change* and the romance *Training for Love*. She has published stories in *The Massachusetts Review*, *Tahoma Literary Review*, *Sequestrum*, and other print and online periodicals. She has been awarded the *Lascaux Review* Fiction Award, *Arcturus Review*'s Al-Simāk Award for Fiction, the Betty Gabehart Prize from the Kentucky Women Writer's Conference, and multiple Pushcart Prize nominations. She's lived in Boston, Chicago, and the wilds of Florida, but her home is wherever her wife, Anna, is.

Playing with Fire

Amanda Kabak

BELLA
BOOKS

2023

Bella Books, Inc.
P.O. Box 10543
Tallahassee, FL 32302

Printed in the United States of America on acid-free paper.

First Edition - 2023

Editor: Ann Roberts
Cover Designer: Heather Honeywell

ISBN: 978-1-64247-463-3

PUBLISHER'S NOTE

Acknowledgments

I was born to a family of "indoor cats," and I considered myself firmly in their ranks for a long time. It may have taken a while, but I busted out through the screen door and fell in love with hiking and natural greenspaces a couple decades ago. To me, there is nothing like being away from noise and glowing screens, to move from one place to the next under your own motive power, under the dappled canopy of trees or along a string of balds with the wind blasting in your face. Your mind becomes free, soothed by the repetition of your steps and the undeniable fact that there is nothing between you and the mostly unspoiled elements.

I also happen to like cooking, eating, and writing about food, so I was pleased when I came up with an idea that could put these two passions of mine together. Food brings us closer to each other, and eating it in the great outdoors makes it taste even better.

Special thanks to the Pisgah National Forest and the Dupont State Forest in western North Carolina for being the perfect playground for me and my hiking boots. From waterfalls to breathtaking overlooks, the southern Appalachians have it all and were a great inspiration for this book.

As always, thanks to Jessica and everyone else at Bella for continuing to support me in this aspect of my writing. I am an incredibly solitary writer, but I always appreciate feedback from good editors, so thanks to Ann Roberts for immersing herself in this imaginary world and making sure I was moving along on the right trail.

Anna, I am in debt to the universe for bringing you to me all those years ago. You're the best partner I could ever ask for, and there's no one I'd rather be with on the side of a mountain, chasing down the last rays of the day.

Dedication

For Anna, of course.

CHAPTER ONE

My mom took a long time to stop worrying about my playing with fire. Then again, maybe she'd never stopped but just learned to keep her worries to herself, knowing how this penchant of hers served only to make me more reckless. She wasn't objectively overprotective, but I chafed at any hint of concern from her, which probably wasn't what she had anticipated when she'd decided to have me on her own when she was just shy of forty. I suspect she'd envisioned…well, honestly, I wasn't sure what she'd envisioned, though I'd put good money on her not envisioning me: destructively strong-willed, according to all the authority figures in my checkered youth; a little hazy on the gender spectrum; and decidedly queer. Mom was a good sport, though, and her career in nursing had come in handy on more than one occasion when my "exuberance," as she called it with one of her many grimaces, got out of hand. It had been just her and me my whole life, and we loved each other to distraction despite our many differences.

Admittedly, my fascination with flames of all kinds had held a heavy bent toward pyromania when I'd been younger, but it hadn't taken *that* long to channel it into service to my true love: food. Was there anything better than the just right amount of char? The way it deepened flavors already inherent in ingredients and added another layer of savory bitterness? The heat and sizzle? Cooking over fire necessitated the understanding of not just the food but the elements, the temperature of wood and coals, the vessels and implements required not to end up with something that resembled charcoal briquettes. Culinary school had been about fundamentals tangential to what I really loved, and I'd learned the most important lessons while using my personal fire pit in Mom's backyard.

When I'd moved home a few years before and had built it out, she'd given me one of those patented grimaces—crooked eyebrows, curled lips, flared nostrils all packed tightly under her mop of graying dark curls. She'd even gone so far as to make the rounds of our neighbors so they wouldn't call the fire department when I was working back there. At least she saw this pit and my efforts around it as legitimately working and didn't ride me to get a "real" job like what some of my culinary-school friends experienced. Could you imagine? Nine to five in a hermetically sealed office? Or twelve-hour shifts in a fluorescently lit hospital, like Mom? No thank you.

I wouldn't do those shifts in a hospital or office, but I'd do them all the time in kitchens since before I'd even graduated high school. I'd worked prep and on the line, short-order breakfasts, and, after culinary school, a year of sauces that made me want to vomit at the thought of a béarnaise. I'd done my time, for sure, and I loved it—in general. It was just that so much food in so many restaurants was *boring*. But, I mean, every other chef must feel this way. We all dreamed of opening our own restaurants to some degree. Mine would be fire-first, of course, with a cozy interior and a large garden where I'd grow my own produce. But restaurants were impossible businesses, and as much as I wasn't like Mom, she'd managed to pass on the thinnest vein of practicality to me.

I was biding my time, living with her and saving my pennies, learning what I could in other kitchens and our backyard, but I wasn't entirely sure what I was waiting for. I knew I was going somewhere, but where exactly—and when—was more uncertain. For the past two summers, I'd been the camp chef and pack mule for The Misfitters, a boutique wilderness guiding and outfitters business I'd started with my best friend, Lucia, and our third wheel, Venus. We curated luxury adventures for small groups along and around the Appalachian Trail that included manageable hikes and delicious food for folks both inexperienced at backpacking and those who wanted someone else to plan and help execute trips for them. Lucia was our certified guide and safety officer while Venus ran the back office and helped drive us and equipment around to various trailheads.

We supplied all the meals, some of the gear, and buckets of knowledge about the environment and enjoying yourself in the outdoors. According to Venus, this was going to be our big year. We were booked from mid-April through the very beginning of November, and though our work was cut out for us and I was going to be a husk of my former self by Thanksgiving, this season was going to put us on the map and maybe enable us to hire help for the following year. Oh, and finance our entire existence during the off-season. Beyond the excitement I shared with my friends, though, I felt a void of uncertainty. If we had more money and put on more tours, I'd have to bring on another camp chef or two. Though teaching people some of my secrets gave me a little tingle of excitement, would I end up sitting in an office somewhere like Venus? Only get on the trail once in a blue moon?

That churning uncertainty of success depended on having a bang-up season this summer, so I'd been in prep mode since the holidays had passed, squeezing in menu planning and experimentation around the hours I worked in someone else's kitchen to help make ends meet. Besides, I was always trying to save money so I could move out of Mom's house maybe before I turned thirty—or she had to go into an old folks home, she joked. I'd quit the kitchen the week before and had just enough time to get everything in order before Lucia and I hit the trail with our first group in a few weeks.

This afternoon, I was trying to perfect a camp-cooked cinnamon-apple turnover, delicious and delicate pockets of gooey, sharp-sweet goodness ensconced in a pastry crust. The crust was the most challenging part, but I was convinced beyond reason that I could get it exactly the way I wanted on the trail. I'd been wrapping raw pastry pockets in parchment paper and foil and burying them under my coals with an almost religious fervor and crossed fingers. It was the perfect dessert to bake in this ancient way while the rest of dinner cooked above. I could definitely do it in a clay vessel, but if I wanted to make it out on the trail, that wouldn't be available to me. I had to travel light without sacrificing flavor and quality, so if I couldn't figure out how to do it with foil and paper, I wouldn't be able to do it at all.

I was singeing my fingers, unwrapping one charred packet from my newest batch, hoping for improvement over the previous disaster, when I heard my phone ringing from…somewhere. I swore and glanced around, wondering where I'd set it down, which could be anywhere. My phone was not my friend and liked to walk off unattended. It wasn't on the picnic table or the pale corner of the concrete patio. It was probably somewhere in the grass where I'd step on it, but then I felt a telltale vibration in the back pocket of my jeans. I dropped the subpar turnover to the ground between my feet, licked cinnamon-sugar filling from my fingers, and grabbed my phone on its last ring. Mom.

She said, "First, don't panic."

"Mom."

"I'm serious. I don't want you driving over here like a maniac."

"What happened?"

"Promise me you won't panic."

"I promise that I won't speak to you for a week if you don't stop preparing me and tell me what happened."

"Lucia just came into the ER. She broke her femur in a climbing accident."

I was off the phone and in my junker of a truck in a panic-induced sprint after dumping sand over the embers of my dying cook fire. Lucia had been my friend since we'd both been in single digits, but in the smallest nod to Mom's maniac comment, I took the drive to the hospital at a speed just short of taking the corners on two of my four nearly bald tires. I ran from the parking lot to the main entrance, squeezed into a full elevator, and speed-walked the hallways until I reached the last turn to my mom's station on the surgical floor, where I slowed to an amble to fake a nonchalance I in no way felt. I knew I'd get nowhere in the ER without her, not being Lucia's family, but I needed to find out what was going on.

Mom was at the far edge of the station working on a tablet with her head bowed, but her mom radar kicked in, and she glanced up and spotted me before I was even within range of her voice. She checked her watch and nailed me with a disapproving but resigned expression I'd seen countless times before. I shrugged in response. A leopard couldn't change its spots, so why expect it to?

I said, "How is she?"

"I told you not to panic."

"I didn't panic. I just hurried."

Mom studied each of my eyes in turn. I swore she could measure my blood pressure and heart rate just by the exact dilation of my pupils. Of course, that was more obvious in my blue eyes than Mom's chocolate brown ones. Apparently, I'd somehow inherited this color from my sperm donor father. I'd gotten her hair though, thick, dark, and unruly. "I wish you'd be more careful."

"People thought you were reckless having me on your own when you did." It was my standard comeback, and it still made a point even after years of trotting it out like this.

"Those people weren't my mother, who I might have listened to. Or maybe I would have reconsidered if I'd known how much trouble you'd turn out to be." Even though her mom had died a year before I was born, which had been both devastating to Mom and had made her take my conception into her own hands, her smile meant things were right between us again. But maybe not right with Lucia, given where this conversation had started out? As if reading my mind, Mom said, "Harper, she'll be fine. They just reduced the break and put her in traction, but she's going to need surgery and months to recover. We can go down to see her soon, but have you called Venus yet?"

"I…wait. Did you say months?" My friends (and some culinary-school enemies) called me a genius with peppers, but in many other parts of my life and intellect, I was the first to admit I could be less than the brightest bulb. My mom was a surgical nurse. I was edging perilously close to thirty. I knew a broken femur was serious enough to require all sorts of hardware to repair and subsequent rehab, but I'd been too distracted by my (yes) panic to put all of that together into what it really meant.

At Mom's insistence, I found my way to the waiting room to sit with a smattering of friends and relatives attached to other patients under the knife. I still had some time before Lucia was stable enough for me to see her, and I used those minutes to sit in the corner and call Venus, who'd been Lucia's friend from college before joining us in the business. She balanced her work with The Misfitters with other accounting clients, mostly small businesses in the greater Charlotte area. Without Lucia, we were doomed, and the call went about as I had anticipated (dreaded).

Venus made it to the hospital in just slightly longer than it had taken me, a speed influenced by the fact that she was whip-smart enough to know what this meant for us with just the barest details from me. She crashed into the uncomfortable chair next to me, her loose afro bouncing with her movement, and summed up our situation in one word. "Doomed. T, we're doomed."

T was my nickname, one that had pretty much subsumed my given one in all aspects of my life—except with Mom. T for tea, which I drank constantly, always hot, sometimes caffeinated. We joked that it was another thing I'd inherited from my sperm donor father since he was apparently English. I wore the nickname with unwarranted affection and pride; it made me feel like a me that was separate from the kid I'd used to be.

I said "How about we wait until she's out of surgery tomorrow before going completely to the worst case?"

"We're doomed even with the best case. If she just regularly broke her leg, she wouldn't be able to guide in six to eight weeks, and our first group is booked in less than three." Venus was like Mom's sister by another mister—a very different mister. They were both pragmatic to the pessimistic extreme, which made Venus a great business partner but a very poor waiting room companion. I was surprised she even recognized a best case even though I couldn't say she was wrong. "Can we just—"

"Fine, okay. We'll hold off on agreeing on our impossible situation until Lucia can participate with us. What was she doing rock climbing so close to the season?" Her hands were up and open like she was beseeching Mother Nature. "You'd think six months out in the woods twenty-four seven would be more than enough to satisfy anyone. I told you we should have insured her."

"We couldn't afford to."

"Blah blah," which was Venus's comeback whenever she had no comeback, a rare enough occasion that I should have been happy to bring it about, but hospitals were not places known for happiness.

I settled in to wait, trying and failing not to think. The sterile room offered no distractions, and Venus hated when I found temporary fascination in her hair, which was both relaxed and kinky, coils of shiny black informed by her Jamaican mother and Irish father. They were the weirdest couple, ever, but still married after over thirty years, which was matched only by Lucia's very Catholic, Puerto Rican parents and their five kids, of which Lucia was smack in the middle. How could the three of us not be The Misfitters? But how could we remain The Misfitters without Lucia Maria Consuela Guzman?

She was the driving force behind the company and the glue between Venus and me. Mom had piles of gap-toothed pictures of Lucia and me from primary school, and Lucia had hundreds of images of Venus and her at UNC, silly or drunk or traipsing through the woods on trips to the western part of the state or up into Virginia, as anyone in Lucia's vicinity was recruited to do. The woman was silly about trees and trails, boulders and mountains, and everything in between. When the three of us were on trails together, we got no end of looks from other hikers, who were so uniformly white in this part of the country that I supposed we were quite a sight, even with my pale, freckled self.

The one thing the three of us had in common was how we confounded our parents. The most outdoorsy thing the Guzmans did was haul extended family into the same park every year for a massive cookout, covering what seemed like an acre of grass with a patchwork quilt of blankets and towels, little brown kids running everywhere, and me, the token white invited solely for my tres leches cake, which I made pans and pans of in preparation and yet had to keep some aside or Mom and I would end up empty-handed. Venus came from a small family of self-proclaimed "indoor cats," who found their living room couch a far preferable location for parking themselves than the closest national forest.

We'd started The Misfitters with our pooled gear plus generous donations from our perplexed families, who would probably have preferred to support us in something less likely to fail spectacularly. The first year, three of us carried ridiculously heavy packs, lightening the load for our guests, but we still leaned on friends to help us make multiple trips from my garage to the closest trailhead to craft the kind of camping experience people would write home about—or tell their friends about. Amazingly, they doled out five stars and exclamations despite collapsed tents, underdone potatoes, and one unfortunate night without toilet paper that had Venus and me trekking through the woods back to the nearest store to pick up the needed supplies before people woke for their morning bathroom requirements.

In the waiting room, Venus remained buried in her phone, probably tallying up how hard The Misfitters were going to be hit financially in the best and worst cases. I'd learned that numbers were the way she dealt with stress. Lucia hit the trails or went out climbing, and I turned to food. Sometimes, I wondered how I wasn't 300 pounds, but I was blessed (or cursed, according to Mom) with a nervous energy that kept me flitting here and there and burning off the unending tasting of my culinary experiments.

I was about to try not thinking about The Misfitters' future again when Mom found us. "You can see her. From what I hear, her family's on their way and will be here any minute."

Venus and I both read between the lines well enough to know Mom was telling us that if we had anything we needed to talk with Lucia about, we'd better do it fast. Once the Guzmans descended, Lucia would be monitored around the clock by one or another of her countless relatives. I tucked that knowledge away but asked the most immediately important question. "How is she?"

Venus said, "It doesn't matter since I'm going to throttle her for this stunt."

"She's fine." Mom squeezed my shoulder to reinforce her professional opinion. "A little loopy from the pain meds."

"How could you tell?" Venus again, sarcasm lowering her voice.

I said, "Should I regret calling you?"

She sighed. "Sorry."

Mom led the way down to the ER, where we found Lucia flat out in a bed, the right side of her face scraped, her left wrist in a brace, and her right leg in traction. What a mess. When she saw us, she smiled before starting to cry. "Guys, you came! I'm so sorry."

I knew the tears were an effect of the drugs, which meant I shouldn't let them turn me into melted butter, but I was also so relieved to see her alive and in pretty much one piece that I found myself on the edge of crying myself.

Luckily, Venus was sober enough for both of us. "What were you thinking?"

"I know!" Now she was really crying and saying something in such rapid Spanish that I only caught about a third of it despite being relatively fluent. The gist was that she was endlessly sorry, sorry in such a dramatically Latin way that you couldn't help but forgive her. But, if my mediocre Spanish was right, beyond the more and more flagrant apologies was something about fixing it.

"Wait, what?" I asked. "How are you going to make this better?"

Lucia glanced around the room as if looking for spies, but her answer was one word and unmistakably clear. "Mia."

Mia Renata Mary Guzman was six years older than Lucia and had been my personal hero for a huge chunk of my childhood, but I hadn't seen her or heard her name spoken around the Guzman household for a good fifteen years. Mami and Papi Guzman had come to Florida from Puerto Rico after they'd gotten married and had migrated up to Charlotte when they'd had Mia. She was the golden child, firstborn, the first-generation dream: smart, beautiful, athletic. She went off to UNC Asheville on a scholarship and Guzman ticker-tape parade and came home for Christmas that first year changed in a way I couldn't quite put my finger on. Whatever it was, the Guzman adults whispered endlessly about it. After that, she didn't come home again, and the one time I asked about her, my question was met with an icy feigned deafness. Even Lucia wouldn't talk about her when it was just the two of us. She was so neatly and completely ex-communicated from the Guzman clan that I hadn't even thought of her for the last decade.

Mia was the one who had introduced Lucia to the outdoors, having literally stumbled onto the woods outside of town during her stint with the high school cross-country team. She'd infected Lucia with a passion for greenspace and natural quiet, the feeling of moving through the world under your own motive power, deeper and deeper away from the distractions of modern life and into something slower and more nuanced. I remembered following along behind the two of them and Mia laughing at my less-than-graceful progress between trees and over decaying leaves. "Harper, we're never going to see any wildlife with you tromping around like that." But she'd said it with a smile that had melted my middle school heart.

Looking back, she'd been my first crush, though I hadn't necessarily recognized it at the time. That had come a couple years later, after Mia was written out of the picture, and I'd fallen for June Parker and had definitive proof of my ultimate queerness.

But even that was over a dozen years ago, so when Lucia said her sister's name, I didn't know who or what she was talking about at first. "Uh, are you high?"

"I had a lot of time to think when I was waiting to be evacuated."

"Okay, but then you were, like, high on pain?"

Venus said, "Shut up, T, and let her talk."

I crossed my arms and sat back.

Lucia looked at Venus. "Mia is my oldest sister." She turned to me, frowning, which accentuated the scrapes and bruises on her face. "The family stopped talking to her, but she never stopped talking to me. Or at least writing. Emails and texts. I mean, she stopped for a while, years, actually. But then she was back, at least kind of. I'm sorry I never told you, but she made me promise to keep it a secret. She was afraid if anyone knew, she'd be forced out completely, and, no offense, but you're, like, the queen of loose lips. And practically family."

"I would've kept my mouth shut for Mia."

"You would've wanted to but you also would've failed completely."

Venus, ever our pragmatic leader, intervened again. "What does this mysterious sister have to do with saving our asses? And why is she mysterious, anyway?"

"She's a wilderness guru and certified guide, so she could do what I do blindfolded. And she's gay, which didn't go down well with my family—or her, at first, I guess."

Mia was gay? I couldn't believe I didn't know that, had never known that. "But I'm gay!" I said. Unhelpful and known by all, but true. "And your parents love me."

"You're not their daughter."

Before she could say more, we heard the rising swell of the Guzman clan coming down the hallway toward us, and by the look on Lucia's face, I knew this conversation was over...for now.

CHAPTER TWO

It took the rest of the afternoon and evening for Lucia to text us what she knew about Mia in the short gaps between being overwhelmed by her family and being drugged out of her mind. Nothing that she told us was good, and Lucia acknowledged she might not even know some of it for sure, given how young we'd been when Mia's disintegration and banishment had gone down. Mia had gotten wild in college, deviating sharply from the straight and narrow. Plummeting grades, getting kicked off the cross-country team, and landing in the hospital with alcohol poisoning. Then a Guzman intervention that Lucia overheard the first part of until all the kids were sent to their grandparents. When Lucia got back, Mia was gone, with all traces of her scrubbed from the house and no explanation given.

The explanation came only years later, when Mia contacted Lucia after she went to college. Even then, it took a while for the full truth to come out. And why not? How long would it have taken me, if I were Mia, to trust that a Guzman wouldn't cut me out for being gay? But I wasn't Mia, I wasn't a Guzman, and my experience with Lucia's family had always been completely different. They were my aunts, uncles, and cousins. They were noise and hugs and chaos. They were the exact opposite of the sometimes claustrophobic unit I had with Mom, and I craved that.

When Lucia was done catching us up, I opened another text thread for just the two of us. *I can't believe you didn't tell me for, like, a decade.*

She's not who you remember.

Of course not. It's been fifteen years. We're all different. Though Mom always said I'd been born exactly who I was, whether she liked it or not.

That's not what I mean.

Then ???

Shit went down. Rock bottom stuff, as far as I can tell, though Mia keeps things to herself. No one comes back from that to who they were before. Call her and see for yourself.

* * *

Calling Mia Guzman felt like trying to reach someone on the dark side of the moon. Or maybe beyond the grave. I didn't expect the phone to ring, and I certainly didn't plan on anyone picking up. I was somewhat prepared to leave a voice mail after a robotic recitation of Mia's number, but when I heard, "Hello?" in a voice similar to but tantalizingly different from Lucia's, my throat closed up with nerves.

"Hello?" There it was again, that husky voice that sounded either disused or tainted by decades of smoking. Lucia had used her version of that voice to get us out of plenty of scrapes, convincing people over the phone that she was one of our mothers with no problem at all.

I coughed like starting a long-cold engine, which was loud even to me. "Mia?"

"Yeah?"

"It's Harper. Harper Varnham. Lucia's friend?" The line buzzed with quiet for a while until I heard the soft trill of a bird in the background. Or maybe it was from my own backyard. I couldn't tell, and it didn't matter. "Are you there?"

"Is Lucia okay?" The question was quiet and tense.

"Pretty much." I'd barely gotten the details out before she confirmed that the hospital was swarmed with her relatives, demanded my address, and told me she'd be at my door in several hours. As if, you know, I didn't have any place to be. I didn't, but still. I forced myself to mix up another batch of apple turnover filling and pastry cases and built a fire to burn down to a steady state while shaping and wrapping the sweets. The work should have been either meditative or tensely engrossing, but all I could think about was Mia.

Mia was gay and different and somehow still in existence, which blew my mind. I'd been obsessed with her as a girl. If I could have, I would have put posters of her up on my walls. She had a way of being right there next to you but still this mythical being, I guessed because she was so much older but would still deign to hang around with us sometimes. My memory of her was fuzzy around the edges and probably influenced by how Lucia looked now, but Mia's smile haunted the back of my brain like I'd just seen it yesterday: warm and welcoming even when she was teasing me. She'd made everything seem easy; who wouldn't want to be around that all the time?

She'd come back into my mind a few times after the sting of her disappearance had mellowed, once in a dream not long after I'd lost my virginity. (Yes, to June Parker, clumsily, in the back seat of her car.) But also when I'd escaped Charlotte for Asheville and the deeply outdoor scene there, picking up work in this restaurant or that, exploring the mountains whenever I could. I'd been right where Mia had gone to college, but I was on such a different path, not achieving but trying to find a way to live that I could get on board with. Of course I wondered about her then, but life plowed time over everything, and she'd settled to the very back of my mind.

Now that time was swept away, I couldn't get comfortable with myself, not until, over four hours later, I opened the front door to find Mia on my front porch. Seeing her in the flesh dredged her up whole from a fifteen-year-old memory. She looked *almost* the same. Her dark, wavy hair, her large, bottomless eyes, her rounded jaw, but I knew right away that Lucia had told me the absolute truth: this was not the same person as the strong, confident, smiling girl I'd idolized as a youngster. She was a couple of inches taller than Lucia and had the same length hair as she'd had in high school, but most of the similarities ended there. The sight of her, here, was disorienting, and it took a moment to realize it was because the last time I'd seen her, I'd been thirteen and about four inches shorter, not that I was nearly a giant now. We were eye level, pretty much, which was the strangest thing. My nerves flattened me again, but Mia crooked an eyebrow even while she shifted her weight in a clearly nervous way.

"Still living with your mom?"

"Living with her again."

"That's cool."

If I'd expected a happy comrade-in-lesbian-arms—and, let's face it, I most definitely had—I was sorely disappointed. Mia was quiet and serious and didn't seem keen on making eye contact. She had permanent frown lines between her eyebrows and around her mouth, and her skin was darker than I remembered, though I saw a hint of something paler—café au lait rather than black with a splash of cream—at the edge of her V-neck, which revealed toned arms under its cap sleeves. But her eyes were the same, and the same as Lucia's: big and the deepest, most bottomless brown. Though I looked into Lucia's eyes all the time, seeing them on Mia's face made them different from my best friend's. Or maybe it was because I was uncomfortably aware of all the secrets that lurked behind them. Rock bottom stuff? Self-destruction? I couldn't imagine and didn't want to know.

We were going to stand on either side of the doorway forever if I didn't get myself together. But how could I get myself together when she was here? Despite her eyebrow and judgmental opening question, Mia gave no indication of being capable of making the next move.

"Anyway," I said, though neither of us had spoken for an uncomfortably long time. "Come in. Or around to the back, where I'm doing stuff. We can call Lucia from there."

She followed me but said, "No. Not when our family's around."

"It'll be from my phone. No one will know it's you."

"She won't be able to say anything meaningful."

I closed the door behind her and led her straight through to the kitchen and its sliding doors to the patio. "Don't you want to talk to her?"

"Of course I do! I want to go over there, hold her hand, yell at her for being so reckless, and tell her that everything's going to be okay. But I can't."

She squinted in the sunshine when we got out to the patio, and it, added to that short but violent tirade, made her look downright furious, even though furious wasn't how I would have described her voice. To be honest, I wasn't great at understanding anyone but Lucia and Venus, but understanding Mia was impossible. Food and fire were much more my speed, and to make myself feel better, I gravitated toward my buried batch of turnovers, which I needed to check.

"I have to take care of something, but we can talk while I work."

Mia sat in one of the cushioned chairs on the patio, but she stayed perched on its edge, her forearms on her thighs, her fingers loosely intertwined. Every move she made seemed to be a notch slower than normal, which was both disorienting and compelling. I kept trying to square her with the idol of my youth but failed miserably.

I dug around under the now-smoldering fire for one of the four turnovers, which I pulled to the surface with a long pair of well-used and charred metal tongs. I could feel Mia watching me while I checked the time before unwrapping the foil and examining the dessert, gauging the color on the pastry and weighing it in my hand, hissing at its heat. It broke apart, spilling apple-cinnamon filling and burning me even more. I dropped it in the grass and sat cross-legged with my hand in my mouth to wait five minutes before checking the next one. Maybe the pastry needed a stronger flour to be a true hand-held dessert. Or maybe it just needed more cooking time and to cool before trying to toss it around like a football.

Mia was still watching me, her frown gone, at least. I wished hard that Lucia was here to be the bridge between us the way she always had. Well, maybe not always. Mia had sometimes talked to me like I was more than just Lucia's friend. Like maybe I was her friend as well, which had done nothing but inflame my childhood infatuation. Who wouldn't want to be the center of Mia's attention?

"Harper Varnham. You're all grown up, aren't you?"

Grown up wasn't something I was often accused of, and I glanced down at myself in knee-jerk reaction: jeans stretched baggy at the knees, sloppily tied trail running shoes I hardly ever ran in, and a white T-shirt gone dingy with washings that I'd worn in more kitchens than I cared to remember. Then again, I'd been thirteen and a late bloomer the last time she'd seen me, assuming Lucia hadn't shared any photos in their secret years of communication.

I felt stiff and uncomfortable under her scrutiny but I also didn't want her to look away. I cleared my throat, which had gone dry. "I clean up all right, I guess. When I clean up."

"Lucia tells me you're a wonderful chef."

"Lucia told me nothing about you." Not entirely accurate, but what else was I going to say?

She frowned so deeply I regretted not keeping my mouth shut. "I didn't want to involve anyone else in our deception. *My* deception. Besides, there's not much I'm interested in having told about me."

Mia might not be interested, but her frown and overall demeanor sparked some seriously morbid curiosity in me. What had happened to her? What was she doing now that she could be here at practically a moment's notice and save us by somehow taking Lucia's place, not that anyone really could. Lucia was the perfect guide for The Misfitters: knowledgeable, personable, and patient. From what I'd seen, Mia was none of those except for maybe the first.

Making this work was up to me, which was probably giving Venus an ulcer. "So...where are you living these days?"

"Around." I thought she might stop there, which made me want to pitch myself in the fire, but she went on after a long pause. "Seasonal work takes me all over, but I have a cabin a few hours from here that's a home base of sorts."

"A few hours where?"

"In the middle of nowhere, mostly. West and up a couple thousand feet or so."

I laughed, afraid it sounded as nervous as it felt. "Don't tell me you've gone all *Deliverance* on us."

She crossed her arms and sat back. "I prefer my own company when I'm not working."

It seemed like she preferred that all the time, given how forthcoming she wasn't. I itched to let her get back to herself and abandon this clearly harebrained scheme of Lucia's, but Venus would truss me up on my own roasting spit if I didn't try to figure out if Mia was The Misfitters' savior like Lucia claimed. "What did Lucia tell you about our company?"

A smile broke through the default stoniness of Mia's face, and the brief warmth of it snagged on something inside me, like the sun through a magnifying glass zapping wood shavings into flame. "She told me your food was the glue that kept it together." She nodded to my discarded turnover. "That smells better than it looks, by the way."

"Gee, thanks. I'm experimenting, I'll have you know."

"She also said you were an excellent grunt, carrying a beast of a pack. She told me a lot about you guys, and I think it's great how you can each contribute in your own way and make something together. I've never met Venus, obviously, but it sounds like the three of you are a good team. The whole luxury part of it, though..." she twisted her face in a wry expression that raised a dimple high up on her left cheek. "Not really my cup of tea."

As if on cue, my phone rang in my pocket, and it was Lucia. I answered, but I was still trying to work my way through that dimple. How could I have forgotten it? I'd tried to make my face do the same thing in the mirror when I'd been young, though it'd been a lost cause. I wouldn't say I'd been a butterball as a kid, but it was only in the last couple of years that my cheeks had lost their baby fat and had acquired the butchly definition Lucia said suited me. Though what did she know? She and Venus were straight to the marrow of their bones—I'm sure to their parents' relief once they'd met me.

I put Lucia on speaker, getting up to move closer to Mia. "Hey, Bozo."

"Is she there yet?"

"She's right here."

"Mia." Mia closed her eyes at Lucia's voice. "I have, like, thirty seconds while Rose is bugging someone for more water that I really don't need."

"Are you okay?" Mia asked without opening her eyes.

"According to the family, I'm on the brink of death. If they don't relax, someone's going to stop being as alive as they currently are, but it won't be me."

"They love you."

It was like everyone held their breath for a suspended moment. Even the breeze calmed, leaving only a small pop of the fire to fill the quiet. I was missing the window for my second turnover but didn't care.

Lucia said. "Sorry. I told T you can help us. Has she explained things? Are you on board?"

"T?"

"T. Harper."

She gave me another squinty look, and I waved it off, saying, "Later."

"I'm on board. Of course I'm on board."

I said, "The luxury thing isn't her thing."

Lucia's laugh was a hoarse snort. "Color me surprised."

Mia said, "I'll do whatever I need to."

"I know. I— Shit. I have to go." She hung up.

As with everything else, Mia seemed to need time to absorb that conversation. Had the two of them talked over the years or just texted? Lucia hadn't made that clear to us before her family had descended. That couldn't have been the first time Mia had heard her sister's voice since the excommunication, could it? In case it was, I gave her some space and returned to my turnovers, digging the next one out from under the fire a minute later than I'd intended.

I unwrapped and examined it. Better color. Dry and firm on the outside, though hot hot hot. I let it cool, levering it up to check out its underside, which had cooked farther from the source of heat. Not terrible. Not a masterpiece, but it at least looked like it would hold together.

"T?" Mia asked.

That's what was important to her now? "It's my nickname."

Her look had "duh" written across it in bold letters. Mia's face made her speaking almost irrelevant.

"I drink a lot of tea."

Eyebrow raise.

"Okay, I drink tea constantly. Hot tea. Even when it's hot out. I used to talk about needing a tea IV but just because it was fun to say. Mom's only explanation for me is English sperm." I laughed. "I say it's too bad I didn't inherit the accent because I'd be such a hit with the ladies."

At that, Mia looked stricken. Shocked, really. She sat up, and her features froze—but her attention didn't stray from me one bit. I waited, wondering exactly what was going on. She made a low, thoughtful noise but nothing else.

"Wait," I said. "You and Lucia have been talking all this time, and she never mentioned that I was gay? You know what a great chef I am but not that I'm into women—like you?"

Mia said nothing, as usual.

"Don't you think that's a big omission, considering... everything?"

Mia's frown was painful looking and unrelenting. "And my parents...You're close with my parents still?"

This just got way more complicated. How was I supposed to navigate all these landmines of revelations and hurts and make this work the way Lucia had imagined? Though Venus would kill me for it, I said, "Maybe this isn't such a good idea. You're not on board with the luxury part of our brand." Once the words were out, I wanted to knock myself over the head with some firewood. Though Mia wasn't the person I remembered and her silences hinted at her being broken in some fundamental way, I found that I didn't want her to disappear for another fifteen years. Also, I hated the word "brand," even though our brand was to be specifically off brand. What a mindfuck.

Mia finally spoke. "I'll get on board with whatever I need to help you guys. My issues are my issues. I'd do anything for Lucia."

As if we were still actually talking about luxury camping, I said, "It means you have to haul a bunch of stuff around that you won't think is essential on the trail or at the campsite. It means you need to humor people who have never done this before, even when what they're doing isn't hard at all. It means you need to motivate people, not just tell them to buck up. And it means that whatever issues you might have with me, who I am, and my relationship with your family need to get buried where no one will notice."

Mia's gaze was direct but not hard like before. "Harper. T? You've been Lucia's best friend her whole life. I have absolutely no issues with any part of you." But she looked sad when she said it.

"Okay. I just…I'll pull out the rest of these turnovers, and we'll talk about what happens on our guided tours."

"Maybe over a pot of tea, T?"

I was itching for some strong Assam to give me a slap of caffeine and obliterate the sweetness of the turnover that had become cloying in my mouth. "If you're going to say it like that, you should just call me Harper." Or nothing at all.

Mia's full lips pressed together in a painful-looking smile. "Sorry. Everything changes, right?"

While I dug around under the waning fire with my trusty tongs, I said, "I'll call Venus and have her come over so you two can get acquainted and she can correct whatever I get wrong. I'm the chef, pack mule, and general camp lackey, but Venus actually knows how the business runs and more about the customer side of things leading up to the tours. She's the bill collector and traffic cop to Lucia's cheerleader but, you know, in the nicest possible way." I was rambling but couldn't stop myself. Mia put me on edge. I wanted her gaze off my rounded back but I also, too desperately, didn't want to lose track of her again.

That night, Venus and I ate tacos while Mia nibbled on chips and salsa and subpar guacamole while Venus talked about The Misfitters. For two hours, she and I drank beer that Mia didn't touch, and Venus spoke until her voice had gone low and hoarse and the beer did nothing to get the words flowing freely again. She covered some of our history and whatever policies and procedures we had in place, with me mostly playing sidekick and peppering all that dryness with small stories of our early trips and trail shenanigans. We finally said goodbye to the mystery sister, as Venus called her in our texts together, and watched her walk down the street away from my house, a small hiking backpack slung over one shoulder. When she turned the corner at the end of the block and disappeared from sight, Venus asked, "Where's she going?"

"I have no idea."

"How'd she get here?"

I shrugged.

She whacked my arm. "God, T. What good are you? Don't you think one of us should have offered her a place to stay?"

"Don't you think she would have just said no?"

Venus closed the door and leaned back against it. "Are you sure she's really a Guzman?"

"I know, right?" Every once in a while, I thought I'd caught a spark of the Mia I'd known before—or known as much as a thirteen-year-old could know a high school senior, but I'd told myself it was wishful thinking. Still, in those rare times when we got a smile out of her, usually in response to some silly Lucia story, I couldn't get myself to look away.

"Do you think this is going to work?"

"Doesn't it kind of have to?"

"No, T, it doesn't. Isn't it better to cancel because of something like an acts-of-God clause than to go forward and give our customers a bad experience?" Venus squeezed her forehead in the vise of her middle finger and thumb, the pressure changing the color under her unpainted nails from a creamy white to deep red. "I know Lucia wants to make things right, and maybe she wants to do something for Mia, who clearly needs something done for her, but all these touchy-feely wants could tank our business just as it's really getting started."

"I know," I admitted, miserable with doubt.

Venus looked around at the door as if she could still see Mia out there. "Do you think she's going to sleep in the park or something?"

"No, of course not." I sounded way more confident than I felt. "But if there's one thing she made clear this afternoon, it's that she values her privacy. I think she spends a lot of time alone in a cabin in the woods."

Venus glared at me, her forehead grooved with what Lucia and I called her "Whatchoo talkin' about, Willis" expression. "That makes me feel a whole lot better about having her be the face of the company for this season."

"Hey, I'm going to be there the whole time. I'll make sure I'm on the trail with her more and that I really work the campsite. Everyone's going to be all high on oxygen and natural beauty, not to mention exhausted by the hiking itself, to be too concerned with Mia's…interaction style." Even I winced when I said it. "She wasn't always like that, you know? She used to be the best thing ever. Magnetic and fun and as warm as a campfire."

Venus snorted out a breath. "You had a huge crush on her when you were a kid, and she's Lucia's long-lost sister. You guys aren't going to listen to reason, are you?"

"I can be reasonable."

She just rolled her eyes at me.

CHAPTER THREE

The next morning, I sat at the breakfast bar in the kitchen and slurped down some cereal, checking the time every thirty seconds so I wouldn't be late to meet Mia at The Misfitters' storage unit. We were supposed to work together pulling out gear we were going to need for the first tour, dragging it over to my house, and assessing and making whatever repairs were necessary. In between bites and watch checks, I texted Lucia. She was recovering from her surgery which had, in her terms, made her the bionic woman, and we interacted in coded messages about Mia so her family wouldn't suspect anything if they were reading over her shoulder. In my messages, Mia was my gold-standard chili recipe, which I didn't even cook at campsites anymore since it was more of an old standby than the fancier stuff we'd trained our guests to expect.

Me: *The chili definitely doesn't have the same kick as it used to*
Lucia: *Maybe it needs to simmer more?*
Me: *Venus is worried that it's going to turn someone's stomach*

Lucia: *Venus worries that the Earth is going to stop rotating*

Me: *Something seems fundamentally different*

Lucia: *What do you expect after putting it through the pressure cooker?*

Me: *It's like it doesn't know what it's supposed to be. It's like it didn't even know I was the kind of chef I am. Like it thought I ate meat but turned out to be a vegan.*

Lucia: *I doubt the chili cares about your dietary preferences*

Me: *If I were chili, I would care if someone wanted me to be meat chili or vegetarian chili, especially if I had a thing about vegetarian chili.*

Lucia: *I'm going now. You're making my head ache worse than my leg*

I slapped my phone down on the counter and took an enormous bite of shredded wheat just as Mom walked into the kitchen. She'd come home after Mia had left the night before, which was good because I wasn't sure how much of a secret I was supposed to be keeping about the mystery sister. I assumed Lucia was managing things with her family somehow, but I'd been deemed an irresponsible blabbermouth already, which would only be confirmed if I spilled everything to Mom.

"Lucia?" she asked, nodding at my phone while pouring herself a cup of coffee. What a terrible beverage, a blast to the taste buds. I used coffee grounds in rubs and marinades, and I made sure I could produce top-notch brews on the trail, but drink the stuff? No way José.

"I need to visit, but going to see her is like trying to get an audience with the Pope given all the Guzmans around her."

"They're a very loving, tight-knit family. Not that I have to tell you. I think you spent more time at their house than here while you were a teenager."

And right after Mia had been banished. "Yeah, well maybe they're not as great as you think."

Mom paused mid-sip and looked at me.

"I'm just saying. Every family has skeletons." I made a wavy hand gesture to soften my implication.

"Which we all should let lie, generally. Though now I'm curious what you think you and I are hiding from the world." Her smile wasn't its full wattage, but she'd just woken up.

I laughed. "Probably just the amount of Stouffers lasagna you made for us when I was growing up. I'm pretty sure I'll live to a hundred and twenty from all the preservatives you pumped into me at such a formative age."

"You can thank me later. In fact, I should thank myself for ensuring you'll be around to care for me in my feeble decline."

I put my spoon down, serious. "I'm not going anywhere, Mom."

"Yeah, well maybe you should. When was the last time you were on a date?"

"I could ask the same of you."

"I'm not nearly the hot commodity my daughter is."

Now I really laughed. "Yeah, right. I don't know which is worse, you having no dates because you don't even try or me trying and failing miserably."

"Someday your princess will come."

"Yeah, yeah. Princess will be a real stretch, though."

Mom squeezed my shoulder and headed back upstairs to get ready now that she was armed with her coffee. My princess. Ha. No one, princess or frog, wanted to date someone who practically lived in the woods for half the year and spent the rest of it living in her mother's guest room in a way that was supposed to be temporary but was turning into anything but. Before that, I'd spent twelve hours a day in one kitchen or another. I loved what I did and loved even more doing it with Lucia and Venus, but Venus was already married and Lucia had always been more of a tomcat around town than I ever was. She had no problem finding guys who would help her scratch the itch of loneliness.

When I wasn't hiking or cooking or gearing up for my next trip or meal, loneliness wasn't just an itch; it was a full-blown case of poison ivy. How did Mia survive out in the woods all alone? Or did her privacy include someone else? A pang of jealousy I wanted to disavow sliced through me, and I picked up my spoon and shoveled another mound of soggy wheat into my mouth to keep myself from thinking about it. But it didn't keep me from checking my watch again and picturing Mia as she'd stood on our porch less than twenty-four hours ago, a living, breathing bundle of contradictions I was way too intrigued by for my own good.

An hour later, I stood in front of our ten-by-ten storage unit and lowered the rusted tailgate of my truck. I watched Mia stroll up the long aisle of closed garage doors toward me. "Don't you have a car?" I asked when she got close enough for me not to shout. "Or did you walk down from the mountain to get here?"

She hesitated at my question, giving a little stutter step that marred the smooth stride I'd been watching. "I left my Jeep at the motel." She shrugged and shoved her hands farther into the pockets of her pants, which hung on her hips, secured by an old black belt. "I like to walk."

I didn't even try to guess what motel she meant and how far it was from here. Despite my texting with Lucia earlier, Mia wasn't like any chili I'd ever encountered; I understood food, but I doubted I would learn to understand Mia or figure out how to work around the fact that she'd been banished while I'd been allowed to stay in her family despite our mutual "condition." Instead of continuing the conversation, I opened the overhead door to our unit, which was crammed to the ceiling with The Misfitters' equipment, both in stacks on the floor and resting on chunky plastic shelves, warping the centers under their combined weight. Boots, packs, tents, poles, waders and gaiters, headlamps and hats, and a whole pile of lightweight but durable cooking and eating implements. Mia peered in and whistled softly. "It looks like REI threw up in here."

"I wish. Most of this stuff is a use or two from the end of its life, but we patch and clean and shine it all up so our customers won't notice too much."

"Is that really 'on brand?'" Mia's voice was so thick with sarcasm it dropped her tone a half octave.

I leaned against the side of my truck, which was like the automobile equivalent to this gear: trustworthy and well used.

"Secretly our brand is whatever we can make work. Half of what you see was donated, the other half was our personal accumulations, supplemented by whatever new gear we could find on sale."

Mia wandered into the small center aisle ahead of me, her hands trailing over lanterns and twenty-four-roll packs of toilet paper. "So, Lucia wasn't kidding when she said most of the people you guide are inexperienced."

"We try to make sure they've done some hiking before or are in decent enough shape to keep up on the trails, but a lot of them haven't ever camped. We don't want lack of gear to stop people from experiencing what we have to offer. Or from paying us for the perfect introduction to the outdoors experience."

She glanced back at me over her shoulder. "You sound like the consummate salesperson."

"No one gets away without selling in such a small outfit, but Lucia's the perfect spokesperson for us. People can't resist her smile and positivity." Which was exactly how Mia used to be but wasn't anymore. Having her here made me realize how much Lucia had grown up to be like her. A ready grin, boundless energy, that truly welcoming vibe, but now, all I felt from Mia was a thick chill. How was this ever going to work?

Mia turned around when she got to the back of the unit. "I'm in charge of gear, orientation, guiding, and safety?"

"We're all in charge of gear, but, yeah, you'll bear the brunt of the rest. I'll be on the trail with you for maybe half of it, but I have to spend time at camp to set up and prepare meals while you do a bunch of the guiding. If it's a big group, Venus will come out and help us, but she's busy in the office and meeting me with supplies at convenient trailheads so my pack can be somewhat reasonable."

"Sounds like you need more people."

"Need is miles away from being able to afford them. We were counting on this season to go well so we could staff up for next year, but Lucia…" I shrugged and shook my head.

She nodded, her face shadowed in the unit so I could only see her chin, which hinted at a frown. "And I'm not remotely part of the plan."

What I really wanted to know about Mia but had no clue how to find out is if somewhere under her spikey, forbidding exterior lurked the delightful warmth of her old self. Was she a Malaysian rambutan or an asam paya? One fruit was prickly on the outside but sweet on the inside, and the other's scaly exterior hid a sour flesh. Just like the distance between what the company needed and what we could fulfill, the gulf between what I wanted to understand and what I actually knew yawned too widely to do anything about. I pulled my phone out of my pocket and looked up the details of our first two tour groups to inform the inventory we needed to haul out of storage and back into the light of day.

Mia walked toward me, the sun making her squint. "What do we do now?"

I didn't know, but I couldn't let that stop me. "Load up the truck."

Back at home, we dragged everything out and into the yard: tents, packs, poles, tarps, solar showers, you name it. Though we never put anything into storage wet or dirty, it all had to be aired out, hosed off, and examined. Usually, Lucia, Venus, and I would make a social day of it, go through a pitcher of sangria, turn the music up, and annoy the neighbors with our singing and laughing, but Lucia was laid up, Venus was tied up, and Mia didn't drink or even talk much, for that matter. I wasn't even making my traditional spit-roasted chicken that we would fall on in the early evening like we hadn't eaten for days, foregoing plates while we sat on the grass and gnawed at drumsticks and wings, licking herbs and oil and bits of char off our fingers between bites.

Still, I kept glancing at Mia, who was admirably intent on whatever task I'd given to her, moving from hosing off and repairing tarps to examining tent poles for cracks or kinks, to counting and reallocating tent pegs. She moved in a competent, unselfconscious way I wanted to emulate but knew I couldn't pull off, squatting and rising and bending with ease, slices of pale midriff showing when raising her arms over her head to shake out canvas and nylon. She acted like I didn't exist, like she couldn't feel my gaze wandering to her too often, taking in her trim shoulders and back, her graceful neck and collarbones, her incredible stillness when she held equipment up to the sun to see it clearly. It felt almost like I was imagining her.

At least until she turned around and caught me staring. "What?" she asked, but it was quiet and interested, not mean.

"Nothing." I turned back to the stack of enamel-coated steel tableware that was a pain in the ass to haul to campsites but that people lost their shit over compared to the more portable plastic alternatives. Every ounce of gear had to get carried by someone, and that someone was often me.

"Harper."

How many times had I heard her say that name when I was a kid? She'd always been laughing when she'd said it, following it with, "*Bobo de la yuca.*" And yeah, I had been kind of a kook. To dispel those memories and reaffirm (at least to myself) who and where I was, I said, "Call me T."

"Fine. T. I can feel you thinking over there, so just come out with it already."

It? As if I had only one question? "Nothing. Forget it."

She sank down cross-legged on the grass in one graceful move, her pants stretched tight across her knees, and motioned to the single-person tent she was working on. "Did Lucia get this for you guys?"

"No, that used to be my personal one. We have a single woman on the second tour who'll need it. Or," I frowned, thinking. "I guess I'll use it again. Lucia and I generally share on trips to save a pound or two on gear, but…anyway." Lucia and I were usually too tired to do much more than whisper about some people in our tour groups before zonking out next to each other in our sleeping bags, but I couldn't imagine lying that close to Mia in a sheath of nylon.

"It's a newer version of the one I used on the Appalachian." She sat still and waited.

Since the Appalachian Trail was practically in our backyard, I didn't think anything of it until the tent and her seriousness combined into a nascent understanding. "Oh," I said. "Did you hike through it? The whole thing?"

"Yes and yes. Once northbound and once southbound. In consecutive years."

I could feel my mouth hanging open, catching flies Lucia would say (and Mia used to), but I couldn't stop it. "That's a lot."

She nodded.

"Like a crazy lot."

"I had some stuff to work out."

"More than four-thousand miles of stuff?"

"Honestly, that probably didn't even cover it, but I didn't have enough money to do it again the next year. I thought I was walking through my problems, but I was probably just trying to outrun them." She looked at me, steady and unblinking, clearly waiting for something, but what? I didn't trust this still-veiled unveiling, and I didn't want to ask something she wouldn't give me the answer to, which seemed like pretty much anything I could think of.

"Don't worry," I finally said. "Lucia didn't tell me any of your secrets. Just that you went through some stuff, had a hard time, and, you know, that you're gay and all." It took all my strength not to roll my eyes at myself. "Not that any of that is necessarily related."

Her gaze didn't waver, and I got squirmy under her scrutiny. The woman had clearly spent too much time alone—either at her cabin or on the trail for months out of the year. I felt like somehow *I* was the foreigner speaking in a language different from everyone else that she couldn't understand when *she* was most definitely the odd one here.

Because I was never one who could hold my tongue when I should, I said, "She told me it wasn't her story to tell, so don't worry about it. I'm not asking you to tell it, either. It's fine if you want to keep yourself to yourself. I'm not going to pry. Just try not to freak out our guests. Maybe smile every once in a while or something."

Her face softened at that, though it wasn't a real smile. "Ah, Harper. Sorry. I mean T. How have you managed not to change at all in the last fifteen years?"

"My mom says I have a maddening consistency."

"I wouldn't call it maddening." She got up with the same economy of movement she'd used to sit down in the first place. "We have a lot of gear to go through. And I guess I need to practice being human again." She started breaking down the tent she'd just erected. My tent. Ultimate proof of my single existence, which was maybe as alone as Mia's, just in a different setting. She bent and twisted, tackling the gear with expertise, but I couldn't help but notice the way her hiking pants hugged her butt and thighs or the thin bra strap that peeked out of the wide neck of her T-shirt. Watching her made me feel like a peeping Tom, but I couldn't stop. She'd invited me to ask, and I hadn't, so it was my own damn fault if I drowned in my curiosity.

Before the moment was completely obliterated, I said, "What was your trail name?" Almost anyone who through hiked one of the three major trails in the country—the Appalachian, the Pacific Crest, or the Continental Divide—was given a name by their fellow hikers that referenced something indelible about their personality or gear or just way of being. Something like "Bubbles" or "Kale" or "Slip Knot." Mine would undoubtedly be T.

She glanced at me over her shoulder, half torqued while reaching for a tent pole. I saw her back expand with a deep breath before she said, "The Orphan."

Regret tasted like ashes in my mouth.

Hours later, I seriously mourned not having made my roast chicken even under these extenuating circumstances. Nothing filled silence like crackling skin and sizzling fat over the snap and pop of a wood fire. Besides, it would have given me something to focus on aside from Mia, who hadn't said a word since answering my ill-advised question. Not to mention the fact that I was getting hungry.

"Food?" I asked.

"Only if you're eating. I'm fine otherwise."

"I'm eating. I'm more than eating. I'm cooking. Do you have any preferences?"

"Don't put yourself out for me."

I shoved my hands in my pockets. "Cooking is like breathing; it's no trouble."

"Does it become trouble if I tell you I'm vegan?" Maybe Mia had been practicing her smile during the afternoon because the question came with a wry little twist of her lips that hooked something vital in my chest.

I hummed, flipping through my internal rolodex of recipes to distract myself from the flutter of my heart at the curl of Mia's mouth.

"That sounds like a yes."

"Not trouble, but a wrinkle. I'll figure something out. Excuse me." I went inside, fumbling a little with the sliding glass door before making sure it was closed securely behind me. I opened the fridge and stood within its chilly light, scanning the shelves without seeing them. What was going on with me? Food, I told myself. Food made sense. Food was predictable, safe, and comforting. As much as I enjoyed my roast chicken and (patent-pending) Huevos Campcheros, I loved cooking with vegetables and grains. I'd hiked plenty of trails with carrot tops sticking out of my pack, a walking, talking grocery bag.

I could whip together a curry or chickpea stew or even a gnocchi and greens recipe that was comfort food on par with chicken noodle soup. I could throw together a Greek salad with fresh dressing or even just a load of pasta if I were feeling lazy. Or lentil sloppy joes. Barbeque black bean burgers and slaw. A lazy Susan of potential dishes rotated through my mind while I let all the cold out of the refrigerator, recognizing my indecision as having nothing to do with food preparation. Mia made me uncomfortable but not in an easily understood way. It would be simpler if none of her was familiar. Or, as Venus had said, if I hadn't idolized her when I'd been a girl.

I had to make this work. Lucia and Venus were counting on me. But how could I make it work when I could only walk on eggshells around her? Or not eggshells, given her veganism. Shards of glass. Splintered wood. A brokenness that was so overwhelming I felt it in myself, and it made me doubt everything. I closed the fridge and leaned against it, pressing my forehead against a receipt for something Mom had tacked up there. Shored up by a few deep breaths, I stuck my head out the sliding door and said, "I have to run to the store for some things. I assume you haven't lost your taste for spicy food?"

"Luckily, some things never change. But we can just order in if you want."

"It's no problem, really. I'll be back in a jiffy."

She gave me a small salute and went back to hosing down some sleeping pads. I left her there with my lie between us. Jiffy wasn't at all right, not when I was planning on heading by the hospital to see Lucia and soak up some Guzman love before setting foot in the grocery store. I'd taken this drive countless times, with and without Mom, and, miraculously, only having to rush once, when a whole cascading series of mishaps left me with a burned hand, lacerated forearm, and sprained ankle—a situation I was sure never to repeat, given how much hell Mom had given me about almost killing myself yet again in my pursuit of open-fire cooking.

Lucia's room was quiet compared to the day before; only her mom, aunt, and two of her cousins lounged around in chairs and at the foot of her bed, away from where her injured leg was. "Hey," I said when I poked my head around the doorframe.

I was greeted with a chorus of Guzman smiles and my name. Harper, not T, which was all right with me. Besides Mom, only they got to call me that, partly because I could never in a million years get them to call me anything else. I accepted hugs all around, though I couldn't help but notice how Lucia watched me move through the room, a question she couldn't ask in her raised eyebrows. All at once, I felt guilty, coming here exactly for this warm welcome, one Mia had been deprived of for half her life. I didn't know the whole story but had now spent plenty of time guessing at it, hypotheses heavily informed by coming-out horror stories I'd read and been told over the years. They shunned Mia but hugged me just because I wasn't a blood relative? If that were truly the case, it was wildly unfair, and yet I opened up and relaxed among Lucia's family, came back to myself in a fundamental way.

If I'd deluded myself into thinking Lucia and I would have a chance to talk during this visit, I had to face the truth. I wasn't here to talk about Mia but to completely avoid talking about her—though there was no avoiding thinking about her. I got the update on Lucia's condition, a recap of all the hand-wringing they'd gone through the day before, a rundown of what they'd all eaten and how good or bad it'd been. Besides Mom's voice, *this* was the soundtrack of my existence. I kept an eye on my watch, counting back from when my food should be ready through shopping and prep time, calculating the last moment I could leave and then adding ten minutes to it.

But before that time came, Mom showed up. "I think I told you no more than two visitors at a time." She said it with a smile, though, and a wink. "You all don't want to get me in trouble here, do you? Besides, it's time for me to take vitals and repack the incision, and I doubt Lucia wants an audience for that."

"No, definitely not. But maybe you guys can pick up something for me to eat so I don't have to suffer through a hospital dinner?"

The food here wasn't actually all that bad, but I couldn't blame Lucia for asking for something different. Part of my love for cooking had been forged in the Guzman kitchen, which always smelled spicy and savory and was warm with conversation and activity. They took their time leaving, and I was right behind them at the door when Mom said, "I'll give you two five minutes to talk, but then I do need to do my checks."

I should have been happy about the arrangement but felt caught out and wondered how much Mom knew about what was going on. Maybe Lucia had told her about Mia, but wouldn't she have mentioned that to me? I slunk back to the chair closest to Lucia's bed, sat down, and leaned in.

Lucia started. "How are things going with her?"

"Fine."

She laughed.

"Listen, Venus is freaking out enough for all of us."

"Then why do you look like they just ran out of your favorite spice at the grocery store?"

The problem with best friends was how impossible it was to hide anything from them. "Luce, she didn't even know I was gay. How could you not have told her that? Didn't you think it was, like, critical information?"

Lucia folded her arms across her chest. "I didn't know how she'd take it. We don't talk about her being gay at all. I never hear anything about girlfriends or anything like that. And, you know, you're still tight with the family, so…"

I put my head in my hands. "God, she's so different. But still kind of the same? I don't know how to describe it, but I don't know if this is going to work."

"She'll pull through. She always figures out how to make things turn out okay."

"Doesn't that depend on your definition of okay? It sounds like she lives in the woods all by herself like some crazy hermit."

"She doesn't stay there all year round. I mean, she has to leave to make money and stuff."

I lifted my head and looked at Lucia, waiting for some better answers. "I don't know what to say to her, and she doesn't seem to know what to say to anyone."

"T, come on. It can't be that bad. Just give her a little time to adjust. She jokes with me all the time."

"In text?"

Lucia shrugged, and I rubbed my eyes hard at that tacit admission. "I just—" I started but cut myself off. Honestly, I didn't even know what I was going to say or if I wanted to say whatever it was to Lucia. Though not saying something didn't mean that I could get away without thinking it. I was afraid it wouldn't work out, but my fear had only a little to do with The Misfitters and this crucial season.

"Give her time," Lucia said. "And don't talk about the family."

"Of course not."

"Or maybe about being gay?"

I rolled my eyes. "I don't have to say anything for it to be completely obvious, you know."

"True enough."

"What have you told your parents about Mia helping with The Misfitters?"

"They've been too freaked out about the fall to really think about it, but I was planning on saying we were getting some contract guides."

"We can't afford that."

"Duh, but they don't know the details. They think Venus prints money out of her ass."

"If only. Fine. Okay." I checked my watch. "I have to go make us dinner. Does Mom know? Can she know? Mia's at the house doing gear check, but I can make sure she's gone before Mom goes off shift."

"I trust your mom with my life."

I huffed out a painful laugh. "Great. Trust Mom but not me with this."

"T, I trust you implicitly now. Mia loves me and you by extension, and it's all going to work out."

"Mia maybe loved me fifteen years ago, as much as anyone could love a punk-ass kid. Now she's suspicious of everything."

Lucia smiled. "Everyone should be suspicious of you, T. Pick the wrong mushroom, and you'll poison us all."

Though it was a running joke in The Misfitters, it wasn't funny now. I got up. "You should call Mia when you can. She needs to hear from someone other than me or Venus."

"I'll try."

"Call her now," I said when I was at the door and left before she said anything or Mom could come back and get me to spill my darkest secrets.

Mia and I sat at the patio table, and I put bowls of gnocchi and greens in front of both of us. The dish was redolent of garlic and thyme with a deep broth undertone. I'd substituted nutritional yeast and ground sesame seeds for the Pecorino Romano I usually grated on top and had added a smidge of miso to kick up the umami a notch. The day had gotten cool while I'd lingered at the grocery store after having lingered at the hospital, and I thought about getting a fire started even though I'd taken the easy way out and made this dish on the stove—and with store-bought gnocchi, no less.

I said, "I know I mentioned something about spicy earlier, but I went in a different direction."

Mia had pulled on a soft-looking flannel shirt and cradled her bowl in both hands, lifting it to her face to inhale deeply. Her cheeks grew dewy with steam, and she made a soft sound. I had a spoon in my dinner like I was about to eat, but I waited, watching Mia out of the corner of my eye while she took a bite, and that sound turned into a hum.

"This is...wow." Another spoonful went down her hatch, and she swallowed and laughed. "It's unbelievably good. Soul-warming good." She looked at me. "How'd you do this?"

"Heat and time?"

"I'm serious."

"So am I, mostly. This was nothing. Or, not nothing," I corrected, not liking how self-deprecating that had sounded. "I used a bunch of store-bought stuff and assembled it. I didn't even make the gnocchi or the broth."

"Or grow the kale, and," she inhaled again, "thyme in your own garden?" She smiled wide enough for that high dimple to make an appearance.

I looked away quickly before I got snagged on its gravitational pull. Her smile was like that hit of citrus you add to a rich dish to brighten it up; it shone through everything right to my most sensitive parts. "I did grow the thyme, but you know what I mean. I can do better. And then you put things over a fire instead of a burner, and it's next-level."

She took a bite. "Har—" she cut herself off after the first syllable of my name, which was weirdly disappointing. "T. This is better than anything I've eaten since..." She cleared her throat. "Well, since basically forever. Thank you."

I ducked my head to my own bowl and mumbled around a mouthful. "It's what I do." But I could barely swallow at the nearness of this Mia that I remembered, the one who had made me want to follow her to the ends of the earth or deep into a forest. I felt myself relax into her proximity, the sounds of her swallows, the little hums she continued to make at the food I'd cooked. We sat in a quiet ruined by passing cars and the distant sound of a leaf blower, background noises that made her silence sit differently from how it might at a campsite, buffered only by insects and leaves rubbing together in the breeze. Or the crackle of a fire. I should light one, I thought, but I couldn't move.

Only when Mia set her empty bowl on the table did I realize she'd eaten the whole thing while holding her dish to her chest, like we'd been sitting around the fire I hadn't made instead of around a perfectly functional table. "I should go," she said.

I checked my watch. Mom would be home soon, putting her feet up and eating some of this stew, which she would say was delicious if she'd had a good day or not as good as the non-vegan version if she'd had a bad day. Ugh. We'd turned into an old married couple, which had been comfortable but was now suffocating. "I can make dessert if you're still hungry."

"If your desserts are as good as that was, I don't think I could emotionally handle it right now." She stood. "Same time tomorrow?"

"I can light a fire. You can hang out for a while."

She glanced down at her hands, which were worrying the open shirttails of her flannel. "I should go. I'll wear out my welcome soon enough. Tomorrow?"

"Sure, but here, not at the storage unit. Venus will be over to review some business-y stuff with you, so, you know, it won't be the super fun time we had today." I dialed up the sarcasm to hide my own confusion at my suddenly intense desire to get her to stay.

She reached out like she was going to touch my shoulder but pulled back before her hand had made it halfway to me. "It was a good day, T. I'll see you tomorrow." She left by the side gate, just minutes before Mom poked her head out the sliding door.

"What're you doing out here all alone?"

I glanced back at her over my shoulder. "Contemplating the largeness of the universe."

"Yeah, I had a shit day, too. Come have a glass of wine with me."

"There's a piece of my lasagna in the freezer you can heat up."

"What about what's on the stove?"

"Eh. You won't like it. An okay experiment but nothing special." I remembered Mia's sounds of pleasure as she'd eaten, and I felt my face grow hot at both the memory and that I was lying to Mom. "I'll be there in a sec."

"Hey, is everything okay? You know Lucia's going to be fine, right?"

"Yeah, I know. Everything's okay. Just tired from dealing with all this gear."

I felt her hesitation, but she finally said, "Take your time. I'll pour you a glass to let it breathe." The door slid closed behind her.

Speaking of breathing, I inhaled deeply and held it for a while before releasing it. Nothing about this was good. Nothing at all.

CHAPTER FOUR

I sat at the kitchen table with my recipe binder and a notepad while Venus hunched behind her laptop across from me. "You should really do something about your posture."

"Don't even," she said without looking up.

"I'm serious. Aren't there, like, gadgets for that these days?"

"Where's Mia?"

"I don't know. Caught in traffic on her walk from the motel?"

Venus glanced at me over her laptop. Her look was clear, and I slumped in response.

"I don't know," I said. "Forget it. She'll be here. Ignore me."

"T."

Hearing my name reminded me of my quickly cooling mug of sencha, and I took a swig from it. "Everything's fine." But then I immediately contradicted myself. "It's just that when I was at the hospital yesterday, everyone was all happy to see me. Hugs and Spanglish and the whole nine yards, which is just...I mean, how can I possibly enjoy that while knowing how they treated Mia for this terrible *affliction*," I rolled my eyes, "that I have, too? And I'm, like, a way bigger dyke than she is."

"Maybe they'll cast you out when you meet someone and get serious. It's easy to ignore someone's deal when they're single."

"I doubt Mia was parading around with some hot girlfriend when the shit went down. It's not fair."

Venus sighed and closed her laptop, pressing her hands flat against its lid. "You say that like fairness is an actual thing when we all know it's not."

No, it most definitely was not. Not to Mia and not to any of The Misfitters and most definitely not to Venus's Irish dad and Jamaican mom. That marriage had reverberated hard through both families, and it had taken years for the affront of their relationship to simmer down to the low level of animosity that still existed between her ancient grandparents today. Of all The Misfitters, Venus was the most attuned to slights and inequity—she was the fairness police, which was ironic since she expected it the least out of all of us. Really, only the fact that I was as big a dyke as I was saved me from the suspicion of being a Karen if I ever put my foot in my mouth, which, of course, I did sometimes. In the deepest, most secret part of my brain, I swore that the intense, bitter-chocolate darkness of her husband's skin was a huge part of why she'd gone out with him in the first place. If there was a stand to take about anything, Venus would at least seriously consider it.

I said, "They *know* how special family is. They go on and on about it, and I get it, I totally do. I buy the whole damn thing. But then they went and took it away from Mia."

"Maybe Mia was okay with it. Not everyone is as in love with the Guzmans as you are."

I trained her own highly suspicious look back at her.

"Yeah, they're pretty great. But if you think it's so unfair you should force them to confront it."

My blood curdled at the thought. "I can't imagine that would go well."

"Then you need to get okay with being a hypocrite and accepting the Guzmans' acceptance of you."

"Thank God you're not our PR person."

"T, I love you, but my mom taught me not to suffer fools, and you're being foolish. We just need to get through this season and back to where we should be once Lucia's on her feet again." She turned to her laptop, signaling that this conversation was over—not that it should have started in the first place. I supposed I should be more like Mia and keep my mouth welded shut.

The slam of a car door made me glance toward the front of the house before shaking my head at myself and flipping through my recipe binder again, trying to find the right menu for the dietary restrictions in our first group, the number of people, the intensity of the planned hikes, and the still-early season, which limited the ingredients I could find at their peak. And now one vegan in the group. I usually liked these kinds of puzzles, but Venus's matter-of-factness across the table was distracting. And the doorbell, when it rang.

"The prodigal sister?" Venus asked.

"Don't be mean."

"Maybe I'd stop if you'd start giving me a warm and fuzzy feeling about her."

I couldn't keep myself from laughing. Warm and fuzzy? Hilarious. I walked through the house to the front door and opened it to Mia. The sight was less disorienting than the first time, but I was far from used to it. Her hair was back in a thick braid, and she wore the same pants as yesterday but a different T-shirt, a baby blue one that contrasted beautifully with her skin and dark eyes.

Beyond her, I noticed an old Jeep parked at the curb. She followed my gaze. "I drove back up to my cabin last night and brought down some things I thought we could use, and I figured Venus would want to see some paperwork and not take my word on certifications."

"Ha. I think she'd be okay, but you really nailed her. Did Lucia clue you in?"

"No. I got a good sense the other night, when she said, 'Lucia and T make me be the adult in the room.'"

"Well, there's that. She's exaggerating, though."

"I get it. We all have roles we play in different situations, but they never truly define us. Unless we let them, I guess."

I hovered inside the doorway, and she stood just outside, her hands in her pockets, her eyebrows pulled together just enough to deepen the crease between them. "You drove there and back last night? Didn't you say it was several hours away?"

She shrugged. "Some nights I don't sleep well, and I prefer to drive when there isn't any traffic." After a quick look back at the Jeep, she said, "I want to help, T. I'm good at helping. I can make this work."

My chest ached at her earnestness. "I've got a killer recipe for vegan pancakes if you're hungry. Most people can't tell that they're not the real thing, though with pancakes, the real thing is such a moving target I don't know how you can compare. Unless, you know, you're thinking about Bisquick or something, which I don't, as a rule." I finally stopped talking and stepped back to let her in the house and back to the kitchen.

"Seriously, don't put yourself out over me. I'm used to feeding myself or making do."

Venus stood when we got to the kitchen. "Haven't you learned yet? No one feeds themselves around T. Not if she can help it."

"It's true," I said. "It's a compulsion. I'm in a twelve-step program for it."

Mia's small grin was more like a frown. "If only all compulsions were that beneficial."

Venus said, "Ready to get at it?"

"I'm at your service."

They took over the kitchen table, and I moved outside, pulling on a fleece against the morning chill. I let myself descend into flavors and logistics, building fantastical menus that I had to pare back to account for reality. This included the availability of ingredients and the potential temperamental weather this early in the season. I was also a factor since there were limits to how heavy of a pack I could carry over this terrain for the average length of our hikes. Oh, and refrigeration, which didn't exist in the woods outside of submerging things in cool streams or lugging around a cooler and a bunch of ice, which was only feasible when we were close enough to a trailhead to enlist Venus's help. A lot more food could go unrefrigerated than most Americans thought, and that was helpful, but mayo would still get you pretty damn sick if hauled around on a hot trail.

One of the campsites we'd stop at was nestled next to a river that was usually like a fish vending machine if I could find the right bait, but I also needed to lug around a backup plan in case they weren't biting. The third site was only a mile or so from a trailhead where Venus would come with supplies that we could ferry into the woods with a couple of trips, so that would be the most lavish meal. Then there were lunches to consider, which folks would carry for themselves but that I still had to make, and make them durable enough to bounce around in a pack for several hours but still emerge delicious. Sandwiches, of course. Cured meats, salt fish, tuna without the mayo, hummus, various nut butters depending on allergies, and caprese on that first day while I could still use cheese. Hell, put almost anything in the right wrap, and it would taste good after five miles and over a thousand feet of climbing.

I had to feed Mia, too, no matter what she said. Besides, I wanted to hear her hum of approval and see her smile with satisfaction and surprise. I wanted to impress her, so clearly I was back exactly where I'd been when I was thirteen. I sighed and put down my pencil. Through the patio doors, I saw Mia and Venus focused on her computer, Venus talking and Mia nodding. I couldn't tell if it were a good nod or bad, obedient or defensive. Or just bland agreement. Mia glanced up at me, and I couldn't look away. I didn't want to look away. If she'd ever gazed at me like this when I'd been a kid, I would have known for sure that I was gay. The pounding of my heart and the excitement clogging my throat would have been impossible to attribute to anything else. Now, of course, this kind of reaction was unhelpful at best and pretty much wrong on every level. Clearly Mom was right, and it had been too long since I'd had a date.

I got up and poked my head inside. "Mia, how much can you comfortably carry on the trail?"

She answered without hesitation. "Fifty is comfortable. I can do sixty without an issue, but I'd get pretty unenthusiastic about it after a while. Seventy is about my functional limit, assuming we're hiking parts of the Appalachian with its technical terrain and elevation gain, and I would require a lot of breaks."

Venus whistled. "T, I think your unofficial title of pack mule might be in jeopardy."

Mia couldn't be more than 130 pounds; we were about the same height, though I retained some of my "huskiness" from childhood in the form of broad shoulders and bulky, muscular legs, and she was downright slender. I couldn't quite imagine what kind of body was lurking under her loose-fitting clothes that could haul a pack half her bodyweight for miles around here and only need more breaks.

I couldn't imagine it, but I clearly spent quite a bit of time trying to because Venus said, "Earth to T. Are you figuring out what weight training you need to do to keep up with Mia?"

I laughed. "Ha. No. Sorry. Just figuring out how that loosens up my meal planning, given that I now have an extra ten pounds to play with."

Mia said, "I'm glad I'm finally good for something." The smallest quirk of her lips hinted at this, thankfully, being a joke.

Great, now I was staring at her mouth, full lips naturally shaded a dusty rose color. "I, uh, yeah, now I really want to feed you some pancakes."

That quirk widened into a grin, small but still noticeable— and effective. "I could eat."

Venus said, "Are you cooking in here? We still have a bunch of stuff to go over and can't get distracted."

We negotiated, and I lost...but also won since I was relegated to the backyard. I built up a fire and set my small cook stand over it while I measured out dry ingredients, dipping back into the kitchen for some spices and almond milk I'd bought for exactly this situation. I tried not to look at Mia during these interruptions, but I managed to sneak glances from behind the refrigerator. She remained admirably intent on working through logistics with Venus. Or maybe she really was intent, and I was the only one of us distracted by the other. That was probably more like it. *Food*, I thought, for the millionth time in my life. *Focus on food.*

The thing with pancakes, especially vegan pancakes, is they needed the just-right heat. Too hot, and you'd go past the expected golden brown on the outside while the inside remained mushy and unset. Too cool, and you ended up with something dry and tough. On a stove, it was easy to dial in the right setting, testing for it by splashing some water into the pan and seeing how quickly it danced around and evaporated. On a fire, it took some finesse and timing. Food was great, and I could spend plenty of time ruminating on it and relaxing into the techniques and skills I'd learned in culinary school, chopping, slicing, dicing, searing, sautéing. But adding in the complexities of fire and the unpredictability of weather elevated cooking to another level of obsession. Getting mentally consumed by it was so easy and satisfying, and that's where I was when Mia touched my shoulder and I nearly fell into the small fire under my cast-iron skillet.

"Oh, shit. Sorry. I'm sorry," she said, eyes wide and fingers splayed out.

I laughed, but it was unsteady. Mom would kill me if I had another careless campfire/cooking injury and ended up at her hospital. "It's okay. My bad. I was distracted."

"More like really, really focused."

"Ha, yeah. I've been told I wouldn't notice a mountain lion nibbling at my leg when I'm in the throes of cooking. It's unhealthy."

"Focus is good, T. Most people never abandon their whole self to anything, but it seems like you do it all the time."

I laughed again and went to wipe my forehead on my sleeve before remembering I'd stripped down to a snug tank top and had rolled up my pant legs while working around the fire. I caught Mia glancing at my arms and bare feet. "Believe me, that's not a common sentiment about my degree of focus." I checked my batter bowl and saw it was almost empty. "Anyway, these are pretty much ready. I'll grab some plates and serve if you guys'll take a break. Is it warm enough on the patio to eat?"

"Um," she said while her gaze traversed me slowly, "you might need some more clothes, but I'm sure it's fine."

"T-minus three minutes, then. You and Venus are in charge of drinks."

"Speaking of T-minus, I assume you want some more hot tea?"

I smiled. "Now you're getting the drift."

She considered me for a long beat. "Do you not like people calling you Harper?"

"No, it's fine. People just…don't anymore."

"So, T is like your trail name."

"Pretty much."

"It describes you and is a departure from your past. It feels all-encompassing, but maybe it's not really?"

I knew she was talking about herself but couldn't figure out if she thought she was talking about me, too.

"Never mind. Pancakes, right? And hot tea." She turned and jogged back inside.

It wasn't long before we sat around the table, my recipe binder and notes taking up the unoccupied fourth seat, the platter of pancakes ringed with containers and dishes of real butter, fake butter, peanut butter, almond butter, my mixed berry jam, maple syrup, agave, honey, and my best Vietnamese cinnamon. Venus had brewed some coffee, and Mia had made me a mug of strong breakfast tea that steamed next to my empty plate. "Dig in," I said and waited for Venus and Mia to serve themselves.

"I don't know where to start," Mia said. "I've never seen so many options with pancakes."

"T only has one setting: overboard. Not that I'm complaining, unless I'm carrying her gear. Her food is one of our biggest selling points." Venus wasted no time snagging a few pancakes and drowning them in butter and syrup, ever the traditionalist.

Mia still hesitated, and I said, "I'd recommend almond butter, cinnamon, and honey, if you eat honey. Agave if you don't, but it doesn't have the same depth. But you can have a second serving with my jam, too. There are bananas in the batter, so you should factor that in."

She followed my lead, and I watched her take her first bite, trying not to seem creepily obsessed with her reaction. Even so,

I got what I was looking for: closed eyes, small smile, and that hum of satisfaction. It made me want to dance, but I restrained myself. I was pulled out of my glee by Venus clearing her throat. She was giving me a very pointed, very frowning look. I made a face at myself and shrugged.

Mia took another bite. "I think you could make me fat if I'd let you."

"Luckily no one says that on the trail," I said.

"Yeah." Venus softened a little. "But over the holiday season, when we're stuck inside, T is one dangerous person to be around. We all start out the new year struggling to fit into our pants."

"There are worse problems."

I said, "Tell that to Lucia. She tears me a new one in florid Spanish every spring."

"Then Lucia's too used to having things so good."

We devolved into eating quietly, but Mia kept sneaking peeks at my paperwork that was splayed out next to her. Eventually, she seemed to be reading more than eating, and I said, "I always bring too much, but we have to handle the worst case."

"I'm wondering how we're going to carry this all. Your weights seem off."

"I freeze dry and dehydrate whatever I can."

"You do that yourself?"

"It's too expensive otherwise, though the freeze dryer was a chunk of change. Venus is amortizing it or something. The whole setup is in the garage, which my mom grumbles about. I've been slowly prepping the staples for the whole season, but today's my last day of freedom before I have to get serious to be ready for the first two trips."

I'd spent the last month buying meat in bulk from local farms, butchering it into smaller pieces, and running batches through the freeze dryer every night. But that was just meat, which Mia didn't even eat.

She speared another couple pancakes and smeared them with my jam. Venus wrinkled her nose. She claimed jam, preserves, and jellies were another English thing I got from the sperm donor. Maybe she was right, but they were still delicious.

The way Mia smiled and licked a gob off her thumb seemed to indicate that she agreed.

She said, "You make these on the trail?"

"A few times a trip, but there'll be plenty of oatmeal, too."

She took another bite and shook her head. "I'm not sure how I'm supposed to go back to trail mix after this."

Venus glanced back and forth between us. "Don't let her fool you, she eats plenty of trail mix, and she always hogs the chocolate pieces. T's the worst when she gets lazy. Kraft mac and cheese, frozen pizza, ramen. She eats like the college student she never was."

I glared at her. "That's enough."

"What?"

"Nothing. Just…nothing."

Now Mia was watching us, her mouth full but not chewing. She cleared her throat and swallowed the bite, which was big enough for me to see her struggling it down. When she spoke, her voice was quiet. "We should probably get back to work."

"Yeah," Venus and I said in unison.

I delayed as long as I could, but I finally had to leave Venus and Mia at the house and go for the first big shopping trip required to start prepping the meals for the menus I'd planned. I usually enjoyed this step, but I didn't want to leave Venus and Mia without supervision. Venus and Lucia didn't make a big deal about my not having gone to college, but I wasn't keen on it being broadcasted around. It was silly because I'd had no desire for another four years of butt-in-your-chair school, but I was also well aware that I'd missed some kind of seminal experience by spending that time both working and screwing around before finally enrolling in culinary school—also a little against my will. I didn't want to be taught stuffy techniques when there was so much history and tradition about food preparation in different cultures, especially in and around fires. But a degree was a degree, and it opened more stable employment for me while I tried to figure out what I was going to do with my life.

For meal-prep shopping, I had to hit three different stores for all the ingredients at the best prices, and somewhere in there,

I was supposed to visit Lucia and try to stomach more Guzman-family love. I put it off over the first two stops even though the hospital was literally right between them, and in the third store, I sealed the deal by buying a load of frozen food I didn't need and that we didn't even have room for at home. God, I was so transparent, even to myself. The whole trip had taken forever because I'd had to cajole people to "look in the back" for things I knew each store carried but that weren't on the shelves. Now it was late, and Lucia needed her rest, and it'd be a whole thing to jostle for position at her bedside around cousins and nephews and way too many aunts and uncles.

Mom and I practically weren't a family in comparison. The two of us, always and by design. No wonder I'd let myself be sucked in by the Guzmans. It had been wonderful to feel loved and yet be almost anonymous: just one of the kids. But I really wasn't, especially not if Mia couldn't be considered one, either. As much as I loved Mom, and as much as I appreciated taking my own quiet walks through the woods, I craved community. I came alive in the bustle of a restaurant kitchen, in the Guzman house, with a group around a flickering campfire. The Misfitters was more than a company to me, and Mia...Mia was so damaged by whatever she'd actually gone through that she spent her downtime alone in a cabin in the woods.

Mia, Mia, Mia. She kept popping up in my mind, even when hauling a sack of oats into my cart or digging around in bins, trying to find ripe tomatoes this early in the season. It wasn't healthy. She was here to help out, still and always a secret from Lucia's family, and then she'd be gone, living her different life and forgetting about her kid sister's friend. She didn't want to coddle our guests, and though she liked my food, she certainly wasn't interested in me. She was interested in walking in the woods—or town, I guess—and fixing things for Lucia. That was it, I told myself. It was just business.

But when I finally got home, Mia was on the patio with Mom. They sat facing the backyard next to each other, a fire going in *my* fire pit, a glass of wine in front of Mom and a tumbler of ice water in front of Mia. Mia was talking, Mom was nodding, and I watched them, heavy cloth bags of groceries hanging from my numb fingers. Mom put her hand on Mia's arm before embracing her around the shoulders. Mia hid her face in her hands, and I backed away from the patio doors, shaking.

This was too much. I understood food and fire and, frankly, very little else, let alone my reaction to that scene. Why was I even upset? I hadn't wanted to keep Mia a secret from Mom, and now she knew. I'd told Lucia and myself that I didn't want to know what had happened to Mia. Whatever was going down out on that patio was none of my business, but I was jealous— that Mia was talking to Mom and not me, that Mom was comforting her and not me, that I was out of the loop in some significant way. I wanted…well, that was the thing, wasn't it? I wanted everything and nothing, which meant I had no right to feel pretty much anything about anything.

I burned off my misplaced emotions lugging bags and sacks and boxes in from the truck, taking over the corner of the kitchen as far from the sliding doors as I could get. I was on the last load when Mom slipped inside, her wineglass empty, closing the door behind her.

"You should've told me Mia was here."

I shrugged.

"Why didn't you tell me?"

I shrugged again.

She sighed. I couldn't begin to count the number of times I'd heard that sound. "Harper. That girl's been through the wringer."

"She's not a girl. None of us are."

"You know what I mean."

"Fine. What do you want me to say?"

"Why are you so angry?"

"I'm not." But I sounded downright petulant, which wasn't going to get me anywhere with Mom. "Lucia didn't tell me about Mia because she thinks I can't keep a secret, so what would it mean if I turned around and told you right away?"

Mom rested her hand on my shoulder. "Mia isn't some game you two are playing."

I rolled my eyes.

"You need to be careful with her. You all do. Can you imagine coming back here after everything that happened?"

"That's the thing!" I said too loudly and hoped Mia couldn't hear outside. "I don't really know what happened, and I don't want to know, not all the gory details. I have an obligation to Venus and Lucia. We have an obligation to The Misfitters. That's all this is about. We get through this season and go back to where we were, and that's that."

She tightened her hand. "Harper, sorry to break it to you, but nothing stays the same, ever. Not from one day to the next, no matter how much you want it to." She let go and walked past me. "I'm going to make up the couch. Mia's staying here tonight."

She said it like it was nothing, and it should've been nothing. It needed to be nothing because in less than two weeks, I'd be alone at a campsite with Mia, sleeping with only two thin tent walls between us. Well, alone plus the dozen or so other people on the excursion. I shook my head at myself. Get a grip, T. I hovered in the kitchen while Mom went up and down the stairs for sheets and a pillow and grumbled at the old pull-out couch. It made a high, soft whine when she opened it. I knew I should go help her or at least do something else useful, but it was too late to cook anything more involved than an egg sandwich or maybe grilled cheese. Besides, for once in my life I wasn't hungry.

I watched Mia through the window, sitting with her head tilted back, face pointed up at the moonlit sky. Despite what I didn't know, I understood what she'd been through in an amorphous way, and what I understood was nothing short of malevolent. I didn't know what, exactly, it had done to her, but what could it have? Nothing good. Everything bad. And it made me…want to fix it, maybe, but also to fix myself. I was still living with Mom. I'd gone from kitchen to kitchen, never quite making the kind of impact I wanted or cooking the food I loved. The Misfitters was great. I loved being with Lucia and Venus, and the work was challenging, but the work was also only half of the year. I wanted more, which then twisted me around to feeling selfish, given how much more I had than Mia.

As if she could read my thoughts or feel me staring, Mia sat up and turned around. She frowned at me for a while, her face dimly lit from the glow of the kitchen. Before either of us could move, Mom brushed by me and came between us, opening the door and saying, "Your deluxe accommodations are ready."

"Should I take care of the fire?" she asked, and Mom turned to me, her eyebrows raised in question.

"No. I've got something to do with it."

Mia came in, and we all jostled around in the kitchen, which was too small to begin with and made smaller by the cache of supplies I'd dragged in. When Mia disappeared out to her Jeep, I snagged a bag of marshmallows, chocolate, graham crackers, the cinnamon still out from the morning, some chili powder I dried and crushed myself, and a box of skewers that I tucked under my arm. I had a hell of a time working the sliding door with my haul, and Mom caught me while I was still making my escape. For the first time in a while I actually felt caught out, doing this juvenile thing just as I'd claimed to want to be better.

"Harper."

"Don't. Not now." I hopped up and down on one foot while trying to use the other to slide the door closed behind me. "Can you?"

She sighed again but came to my rescue.

"Do you want one?"

"Considering my family history of diabetes, no. And you can't run away from Mia's history, just like she can't."

"I'm just having dessert. It's nothing." It was a lie both of us surely saw through, and it was a relief when there was some solid glass between us. Mia must've really rattled her because she almost never talked about family history with me. We both knew what the sperm donor had provided for his medical history when he'd jizzed into a cup, but that wasn't the same as truly understanding what I was or wasn't in store for. It was something Mom and I acknowledged in the most oblique way but mostly pretended it wasn't a thing. And it mostly wasn't. Sometimes, though, it was a reminder of how limited my family bonds were across the board. I was all Mom's, of course, but I was half a phantom who had looked good on paper and partly a self-invited, persistent guest of the Guzmans. I had one foot out the door everywhere, which I guess was better than where Mia was, but I wasn't keen on chasing those similarities any farther.

I stoked the fire and sat in the grass, which was so cool it felt dewy. I basked in the fire's warmth and the ground's coldness and listened to the pop of sap in the new logs that had caught quickly, logs I had to buy instead of gather in our tame, suburban enclave. Charlotte was only a couple hours from Asheville, where I'd felt most alive, but it was a totally different world. Here, it was flat and planned and boring. Mia had been the one to unlock adventure for us, taking us driving to the mountains and trails as soon as she had her license. She'd been my gateway to practically everything worth anything.

Eventually, the cold wasn't just under me but seeping into my back as evening rotated into night. This was my favorite time, when the fire pushed away sleep for a while, when the last log had been placed, and all that was left was to quietly watch it burn down to nothing.

I laid out a graham cracker square on a perfect flat rock ringing the fire pit and set a square of chocolate on it. The chocolate was too nice to be used in this application, but the cheap stuff didn't melt as well. I dusted the chocolate with cinnamon and a dash of pepper, popped a marshmallow on a skewer, and toasted it while the indirect heat had its way with the chocolate. The result was a sumptuous mess even more gooey than most people's versions. Eating it was a little like taming an ice cream cone on a scorching hot day, chasing melting streams with your tongue before they got to your fingers...or after.

I ate three of them in a row before the sweetness overwhelmed me, and I had to stop. The fire was a shadow of its former self, and soon it didn't give off enough heat to keep me warm. My arms were studded with goose bumps when I finally dragged myself to my feet and gave the embers a heavy dusting of sand. When I was sure I wasn't going to burn the neighborhood down, I gathered my s'mores supplies and headed back inside, the coast certainly clear by now, any and all moral skirmishes relegated to the morning.

The house was dark and still, the only light coming from the dim bulb over the stove. I got a glass of water from the tap to wash down all the sugar I'd just eaten, snapped off that one light, and made my way to the stairs by muscle memory. My hand had just found the banister when I heard Mia say, "T?"

"Yeah?" I whispered.

"Did you see Lucia today? How's she doing?"

I gave up on the idea of a quick escape and turned into the living room, where I could make out Mia, propped up on one elbow, faintly silhouetted by the picture window behind her. "I made s'mores and should've offered you one." It was like a drunken confession.

"I can't eat them."

"Right, right. Horse hooves *and* cow juice. It sounds disgusting when you say it like that."

"Is Lucia all right?"

"She's fine. She's grand. She's drowning in Guzmans. Didn't she call you yesterday after I was there?"

Mia slid back down so her head was on the pillow. "No."

"I shouldn't have said that. The drowning thing."

"What, the truth?"

"There's the truth, and there's letting the truth out all over."

Those words sat between us for a while. I couldn't hear Mia's breathing, but when she moved her legs, the sheets made a swishing sound like wind through leaves. I finally noticed that she was looking at me steadily, and I felt my blood thicken. Or maybe it was the s'mores fully making their way through my system.

She sighed. "I'm going to start checking the trail conditions tomorrow."

"I'm going to start cooking."

"And never stop?"

"That's the plan. Or at least the dream, I guess."

"Your mom says you want to open a restaurant."

I huffed out some breath. "Yeah, me and every other chef in the city." I was starting to think I'd said this was my dream because I thought I was supposed to, which was such a sobering thought to my sugar high that I squashed it as quickly as I could.

"Don't do that."

I was going to respond with some sass, but I was suddenly deflated and felt older than I actually was. "Grab whatever you need to eat from the kitchen. We've got plenty of everything."

"Tell your mom thanks."

"Tell her yourself tomorrow. Goodnight."

I practically ran up the stairs to my room. What was wrong with me? Nerves and attitude and this horrible sadness all jockeying for position inside me, making me seem like a damn teenager again, not that Mia had seen me during those years the first time around. She'd somehow escaped awkwardness during her adolescence, but what good had it done her? Then again, maybe it was revisionist history. I was a kid when she left—or was run out of town. I'd idolized her, made her into something she clearly wasn't.

I brushed my teeth viciously, shucked off my smoke-tinged clothes, and slid into bed. Mia's skin had looked like silk when she was out on the patio, her eyes deep pools of dark chocolate. I was jealous of my own mom for being able to touch her, comfort her. She was broken. Anyone could see that. But I could also see these flashes of the person she'd been, and here, alone in my bed, sheets cool and soft against my back and breasts and thighs, I knew what I remembered from fifteen years ago had been every bit the truth.

CHAPTER FIVE

When I got up in the morning, Mia was gone—the bed tucked back into the couch, the sheets and blankets folded on top of the cushions—and she stayed gone for eight days. For eight days, I portioned out oats; my own pancake mix; seasoning packets for my apple turnovers, crumb coffee cakes, Huevos Campcheros, and ratatouille; and beans I would soak and cook at the campsites where we'd stay for two nights because I was a crazy fool. In between, I made large batches of Massaman curry, garlic mashed potatoes, and a basil heavy pasta sauce I freeze-dried to reconstitute on the nights we would hike most of the day.

And in between that, I called Mia and was sent right to voice mail. I texted my worries to Lucia, first in the hospital and then at her parents' house after she was discharged.

I think the chili has disagreed with us.
Indigestion or…?
…evaporation.
???

I've lost control of the spices.

Eventually she called. "What're you talking about?"

"She's gone."

"What do you mean, gone?"

"I mean not here. Not answering when I call."

Her sigh was loud in the phone. "You worry too much, T."

"How could any worry be too much when she's gone off the map? She was just supposed to be checking out the trails, making sure the campsites were okay. The usual pre-season stuff."

"Then that's what she's doing."

"You're clearly still on too many pain meds."

"I trust her absolutely."

I managed not to wonder aloud if that were because she hadn't actually been around Mia lately. Besides, she didn't have Venus up her ass for updates three times a day. Sometimes I was surprised that Venus trusted Lucia and me as much as she did. Suspicion ran as thick in her blood as cumin in my chili—three bean and corn instead of meat, given the necessity of feeding Mia, which I was rethinking more and more each day.

Six days in, Venus and I were brainstorming solutions to move forward without either Mia or Lucia, none of which were good, but we needed to find a way that might allow us to limp through the season without giving refunds or shuttering our doors for good. Going down this road felt traitorous but necessary, and while we were talking, I avoided Lucia as much as possible as well as the rest of the Guzman clan. Have faith, I told myself, but I wasn't great with things I couldn't see and smell and touch, let alone eat, and so I worried and planned, planned and worried.

For those eight days, Mom wouldn't touch me with a ten-foot pole and not just because I was cooking, measuring, and freeze-drying my ass off. I filled the kitchen with loud punk rock music to give my worry the appropriate soundtrack. In other years, I would've found myself dancing around to it while all the burners were going, simmering off restless energy from being stuck inside, but my feet felt heavy and uninspired. The most I could rouse in myself was a violent nodding of my head that tossed my light brown hair in and out of my eyes.

After stirring the bechamel sauce for mac and cheese that was one huge nod to my majority non-vegan crowd, I pushed my hair from my face and saw Mia standing at the patio door, hand raised as if to either wave or knock. My music reverberated against the glass between us, and I let out a very girlish shriek of surprise before slapping my palm over my chest to keep my heart from exploding out my ribcage. We watched each other through thick soundwaves and clear glass, and I was so pissed and happy I couldn't move.

Mia slowly pulled the door open, recoiling at the volume of the music. Her eyes narrowed and eyebrows drew together, deepening the crease there. "T?" I saw my name more than heard it, and that was enough to prompt me to slide over and grab my phone from the edge of the table, where it was nearly lost among plastic bags, spice containers, and my scribbled notes crisscrossing the menu I'd drawn up before Mia had left. I stopped the music, and we blinked at each other.

She said, "I didn't mean to interrupt."

"Where the fuck have you been?"

She stepped back as if I'd hit her. "Checking the trails and campsites?"

Mom's voice came right out of my mouth. "You couldn't answer your phone or call or, like, send a carrier pigeon with news? You couldn't be bothered to check your voice mails or stop by in the evenings between trail sections? You didn't think that maybe Venus or I would want to be in touch in the week leading up to our tour? That maybe we'd have business to discuss or need to know if we had to communicate with our guests or adjust our own expectations or requirements for gear or food? Did you just not think at all?"

By the time I was done, Mia was flush against the patio doors, looking as if she wanted to melt right through to the other side and truly disappear this time. I immediately regretted the tone of my outburst but not the content. Seeing her here, I felt the true extent of my worry for the first time, my overwhelming dread of Mia being out there alone, maybe hurt, dead, even, a dread I had successfully avoided feeling about anyone, ever, not even Mom because where did she ever go, anyway? But it had lurked under my skin ever since Lucia had smeared herself at the base of a mountain.

"I don't take my phone on the trail. I left it in my car at the first trailhead and hiked the full route, like I assumed I was supposed to, then turned around and came back."

"You camped? Lucia always comes back between trail sections."

"I like camping."

We all liked camping, so this felt like the most nonsensical statement. It finally dawned on me that she preferred to sleep alone in the woods than spend another night on our pull-out couch. Not that it was the height of luxury, but it was warm and dry. And I was here. None of which she was interested in at all.

I said, "We're all relying on you."

"I know that."

"We've got enough on our minds without worrying that—"

"That I'm going to run away? That I'm going to relapse? That I'm going to screw this up for you two and Lucia? That I'm going to shame my family again? Join the club, T. But I made a promise to Lucia, and I'm not breaking it. So you guys are stuck with me for now since I'm not going anywhere." But she seemed to immediately contradict her words by opening the door behind her and stepping out onto the patio. "I need to clean my gear. The trails are mostly fine, by the way. One pretty soggy stretch we'll either need to wade through or there's a detour, but it will add a few miles. It might dry out by the time we get there with the group, depending on the forecast, which I'll look at tomorrow or the next day to make a final call." She closed the door behind her.

My heart thumped too hard, making itself known instead of just going about its job as quietly as usual. Maybe it was still the adrenaline from the surprise of her or the last of my anger burning off after my tongue lashing. But it was also because of a hard slice of regret at making her look so sad, cheeks flushed but eyes downcast, chastising herself as much as me for going off on her like that. I wanted to apologize, I wanted to have done better, but I still believed she should've called, should've acted like a normal human being and communicated with us. The pressure of this season without Lucia was hard enough for me to handle; if Mia were as fragile as she seemed to consider herself, what might it be doing to her? Relapse? Into what, exactly?

I didn't want to know, which was becoming an insistent and sickening refrain. The only thing that was certain right now was that she was a good choice to bail out The Misfitters because she was the only choice, and she certainly wasn't a good bet for me, not that I wanted to acknowledge what I meant by that. Keep it professional and get through it. I turned back to my sauce and tried hard to ignore Mia just outside.

It started raining that night and was a steady downpour when Mia arrived the next morning. I was already in the kitchen when I saw her standing amidst the wet gear with her hands on her hips before she knelt to one of the two-person tents and started setting it up. I yanked open the sliding door. "What're you doing?" I had to raise my voice to carry over the sound of hammering rain.

She turned toward me with a hand over her eyes to protect them from the pelting water. "Making a dry space for me to put these four packs together."

Clearly my outburst from the day before hadn't sufficiently shamed me because my tone was still hard when I said, "Pull everything into the garage so you don't have to pack things wet."

"Won't your mom be put out?"

"I've commandeered her kitchen for weeks. I don't think the garage will be a deal breaker. I'll open the door for you." I closed the door and did as I'd said. I didn't offer to help move the gear, and I wasn't sure why. I didn't mind getting wet or doing some manual labor. Though I had plenty to keep me busy inside, I could spare twenty minutes to walk things around the house and set them on the stained concrete of the garage floor. In fact, it sounded like a rather pleasant diversion from more hours at the stove and filling baggies with weighed out raw ingredients.

I didn't do it because I couldn't decide if I felt justified or terrible for how I'd laid into Mia. She'd been both irresponsible and thorough, good-hearted and willful. I wanted to trust her, but I couldn't. It was all too unequivocal, and that wasn't how I operated. Food, I told myself. It was what I was good at, anyway, and I could keep everything under control, even fire.

Sometime later, Mia opened the door from the garage and said, "Hey, T? Do you have a towel I can use? I don't want to drip all over the carpet."

I grabbed one from my bathroom and met Mia at the threshold. She was saturated with rain, her clothes clinging heavily to her shoulders and hips. I was struck with something well beyond the remnants of hero worship, and it took me a moment to hand the towel over to her. "Do you need some dry clothes?"

"I already got some from the Jeep."

"Okay, so…?"

"Everything's fine. I just need to let some stuff dry out a bit before I can organize it and pack it up. We need four packs with the basics this trip, right?" Her voice was muffled as she rubbed the towel over her hair vigorously.

"You'd know better than I would. I only deal with dietary restrictions and preferences."

"I'll figure it out. Don't let me keep you."

"Mia, listen—"

She dropped the towel and looked at me. It was neither friendly nor unfriendly, which was a little unnerving. "Don't worry about it." She melted back into the garage and closed the door between us.

My outburst continued to shadow the space between me and Mia just like the blanket of storm clouds that dogged us. Once Mia finished with the gear in the garage the next afternoon, she sat in the middle of the couch with our camper questionnaires out in front of her on the coffee table. Every time I glanced in at her, she was reading them like they were the holy grail or something. I hoped she was committing them to memory the way Lucia did, but Luce made it all seem much more casual, sharing interesting bits of information with me and Venus while she went through the short stack of forms.

"This guy used to be an Army ranger," she'd say. Or, "You know these two are Kosher, right T?"

Of course I'd known since it had taken an entirely different kind of preparation than I normally had to do—even if I didn't bring anything dairy related on the trail. I needed the right cuts of meat and had to deal with them in a very specific way and it was all super interesting and stressful.

Mia was quiet as the grave, but one time, when I cut through the living room to go upstairs to lie down and rest my back for a few minutes, I caught her sketching in a notebook. Or I assumed it was sketching the way her pencil moved in quick, small strokes that couldn't be confused with handwriting. I stopped at the bottom of the stairs and watched her. She didn't seem angry or determined or shut down or any of the other ways I'd seen her the first couple days we'd spent together. I couldn't put my finger on her expression, but it made me feel calm to look at her—at least until she glanced up from her paper and met my gaze.

Now I felt embarrassed. "Sorry," I mumbled and took a reluctant step up the staircase.

"T, I said don't worry about it. Sometimes you just have to go forward, okay?"

"And you're the expert?" Good God, why was I such a brat sometimes? Even as I was trying to be better.

She laughed. "Not nearly, but I've had to do it a lot, so I know a little something."

I stood, hovering in indecision between making the rest of my way upstairs and turning to engage more deeply with Mia in the living room. I took the cowardly middle ground and stayed exactly where I was. "You should have called at least once."

"I realize that now." Her words were quiet.

"None of us is ever calm before the first trip of the season. It's a million different details to nail so we can get good reviews.

Reviews are everything to us. There's just a lot at stake." I spoke to the stairs in front of me, not daring to look back at Mia.

"I swear you won't have to worry about me again."

I wanted to believe that but couldn't. A twinge in my back made me climb the rest of the stairs so I could flop down on my bed and try to relax.

The night before the tour started, Venus and Mia were sitting at the kitchen table, waiting for me to put my finishing touches on dinner. I always made my chili for this meal since I didn't serve it on the trail. Thick and savory with just the right amount of heat paired with golden corn bread, thick pats of butter, butter substitute, and honey for those of us saddled with a sweet tooth. This time, the chili was definitely not con carne, and I'd used several substitutes to make the corn bread vegan. Long live flax seed as a powerful egg substitute.

I ladled the chili into three bowls, slid a small dish of shredded cheddar cheese in front of Venus, and brought a plate full of corn bread squares for the center of the table. It was so strange not to have Lucia here. Without her, the room had been uncharacteristically quiet through my final prep, and my voice sounded weirdly loud when I said, "Dig in." The room went quiet again as people brought spoons to their mouths, blowing on them in small billows of steam.

Venus spoke first. "Masterful as always, T."

"You're just saying that because you have to."

She laughed. "I'm pretty sure I never have to compliment you; your ego is plenty well developed on its own, especially around food."

"You say such sweet things."

Mia watched us banter but didn't chime in. She did, however, close her eyes when she tasted the corn bread. She was halfway through her chili and her second piece of corn bread when she said, "Why do you guys ask about their favorite vacation in the questionnaire? I get all the other questions, but since the answers are all over the place for this one, I'm not sure what the goal is."

Venus said, "That was Lucia's question, right?"

"Probably," I said, "But we all talked about it before we put it in. It's not about the vacation, necessarily. It's about how they describe it. What words they use and everything. And we want to know because we want them to leave the trail thinking that their time with us was better than that old, stinky vacation. To beat something, you have to know what you're trying to do better than—and what aspects of it were most important to them. Nothing's going to make us fundamentally change our approach to try to win one particular camper over, but we're flexible enough to try to press the right buttons when we can."

"Don't worry," Venus said. "It's not as creepy as it sounds."

Mia put her spoon down and smoothed corn bread crumbs from her T-shirt. "It doesn't sound creepy at all. I think it sounds pretty smart. And this is the best chili I've ever had. Do you share recipes, T?"

A hundred different cheeky responses flooded my brain, but I wrestled them down before saying, "Sure. You're family, right?"

Her frown told me otherwise, but I decided to ignore it. I picked up my own spoon and worked on the last bit of dinner in my bowl, reminding myself that this was going to be the last relaxed meal I was going to have for days.

The next morning, Venus pulled up to the house before the crack of dawn in a rented van big enough to hold the three of us and all but two members of our first group of the season. Mia, who had slept on our sofa bed the night before, loaded her stuff along with mine in the back, as well as the four packs she had outfitted with starter gear and piles of loose gear we'd distribute among our other campers. Usually, we'd be chattering through our excitement and nerves, but it felt like we were embarking on a death march. Venus kept the checklist while Mia and I made trips back and forth. Mia's hat shaded her face and neck from the streetlights with a brim gone soft with wear, and her boots were heavily creased but clean. Since the morning was still cool, she wore a faded tan-and-pink flannel over a gray T-shirt and hiking pants with pockets I knew held our trail maps, compass, personal locator, Leatherman, and a small waterproof container of matches. A cracked but still serviceable belt circled her hips, and I tried unsuccessfully not to check out her behind as she bent to pick things up and pack them in the van.

Finally Venus said, "That's everything. We need to make three different stops to pick people up, two here in Charlotte and one in Asheville, and we'll meet the rest at the trailhead."

Mia got in the back of the van without a word, buckling her seat belt and crossing her arms. When I climbed in the front passenger seat, Venus shot me a look, and I shrugged. It was too late to do anything about anything at this point. But after twenty minutes, we pulled in front of the first house, where four of our campers were waiting outside, and Mia was out of the van before either of us could even unbuckle, a wide smile on her face and energy in her voice when she greeted the nervous-looking women.

"I'm guessing you all are waiting for us. I'm Mia, your trail guide on this adventure. Welcome to The Misfitters! Are you ready to get started on an experience we hope will change your life? Or at least the next ten days of it?"

Venus whispered, "What the…"

My sentiment, exactly. How many times was this woman going to leave me speechless and immobile? Mia was teasing them about their tight smiles and matching names from our roster to each of them by the time I managed to scramble out of the van and hover next to her.

"Ah," she said. "This is our camp chef and all-around leisure director, T. I'm sure you'll figure out what her nickname stands for by the end of the day—or even before we're out of town. I recommend getting on her good side because she's carrying a lot of our food in her pack."

I grinned and waved. "Hey, everyone. No need to suck up. We're all going to eat well on this trip, but if you want to butter me up, I can't resist a good ghost story around the fire at night." After shoving more gear in the back and introductions with Venus, we herded the women into the van, where Mia chattered at them for the fifteen-minute ride to the next stop, where the same enthusiastic greeting ensued.

By the time we'd made all three stops (the second and third separated by ninety minutes of driving) and pulled into the trailhead parking lot, I was completely unmoored, and Venus was grinning, muttering, "It just might work," over and over again in a maniacal way. Mia was the confident cheerleader I'd worshiped as a girl, but it was impossible to reconcile that with the woman I'd worked next to (but definitely not with) over the last few days of preparation. When we found the rest of the people in our group, we gathered around her in a loose semicircle as she gave us our orientation, some of which was familiar from going through the same thing with Lucia many times, but the rest of which was Mia's own spin on the information.

"First," she said, "we're all in this together. T and I are responsible for your overall health and safety, and, hopefully, for providing you with an excellent experience, but because we're traveling as a group, we're accountable for each other. This means we all need to follow the same rules and respect each other and the national forests we'll be traveling through."

She broke down trail and camping etiquette, terrain and distances, and the importance of communication. She was clear about our expectations for them and what they could expect from us. Nothing she said hadn't already been told to them in one way or another with all of the mailings we'd done leading up to this trip—and the waivers we'd had them sign—but Mia commanded the group, holding everyone's attention through their excitement and nervousness. Even after she finished, she wasn't quite done. She had each person don their pack and checked them for proper fit and weight distribution, laying her hands on their hips and shoulders after getting permission and adjusting straps and securing whatever essential or silly thing some of them had attached to the outside of their packs.

I couldn't look away from how she handled everyone, especially the women, who accounted for nine of the dozen people in this group. We had some groups later in the season that were all female, which was one of the things The Misfitters liked to offer, given our all-female crew. Those trips were a blast, with everyone relaxing into being on the trail away from the male gaze, not that men ever bothered gazing at me outside the forest—or inside, for that matter. Though I was hardly the butchiest woman I knew, I was far enough over the line to fall off their radar. But right now, I hated that I wanted Mia to pay attention to *me*, to test the fit of my pack, run her hands under my shoulder straps, give the belt at my hips a suggestive tug, smile and meet my eyes.

After I gave Venus a quick, one-armed squeeze, we were off, Mia lugging fifty-seven pounds and me forty-eight, knowing our weights would reduce over time as our campers started eating through the food we were carrying. Mia took the lead, and I was the sweeper, making sure no one fell too far behind and giving pep talks to folks if they got tired during long ascents or near the end of the day. Even with our later start this morning because of the drive and orientation, this first leg was short enough that I wouldn't have to hurry ahead to set up camp before it got too dark, but that would be my job when we moved our base every other day.

It took a couple of miles, but I finally succumbed to the rhythm of movement, putting one foot in front of the other and enjoying the solid feel of my boots around my feet and the soft air pulling into my lungs. The group had started out chatty, but now everyone seemed intent on enjoying the quiet around us, the flutter of a bird here and there, the soft thump of footfalls onto packed dirt. It was even cooler deep in the forest, surrounded by hemlock and oak, maple and beech, which made the push of blood through my body feel exhilarating. Next to the focus of cooking, my most precious pleasure was making my way by my own motive power over miles of varied terrain with the press of my pack on my back and my muscles working in concert with my breath.

We stopped and grouped up every half hour or so to make sure everyone was drinking and to compare notes on flora and fauna we'd seen since the last break. Mia was a fount of information about trees and flowers, rattling off both common names and their Latin equivalent and filling us with random facts about the codependence of various species in the ecosystem we were slowly moving through. Too slowly by my watch, but Mia was in charge on the trail, and I was still so confounded by the transformation in her personality that I wasn't about to challenge her. I satisfied myself with offering up scoops of my sweet and spicy trail mix that included both curried cashews and honey-roasted almonds along with a warning not to ruin their appetite for lunch. After a few minutes of chatting, drinking, and munching, Mia would lead us out again, and I would find thin comfort in my breath, the feel of my pack on my hips, and the push and pull of my quads and calves.

The thing about hiking was that it brought you outside yourself into your surroundings but also gave you the opportunity to tune in more closely to your own internal experience. I loved being in motion, partly because Mom had taught me to always be busy and productive but also because that was the only way my brain actually worked. Sitting still made me crazy, and my thinking only flowed when my blood was moving. The Misfitters didn't frown too terribly on chatting while on the trail, but we also counseled people that you could miss the best stuff if you wasted all your miles blabbing to your trail mates. Luckily, most folks in this first group seemed to agree except for one couple, who I realized only later were halves of two different couples but who seemed to find each other endlessly fascinating.

About when my stomach started growling, Mia led us off the trail on an overgrown spur I'd never noticed before despite having hiked this stretch literally countless times. After a few minutes and some gnarly terrain that tripped up most of us at some point, we stepped into a small clearing tailor-made for a lunch break with a long, fat fallen tree, a couple of boulders, and a mostly flat expanse of patchy ground cover.

Mia said, "Everyone take a load off while T and I get your lunch together. We can do some introductions while we eat and rest up for the next five miles."

There were some groans at that, but everyone was smiling and shrugging off their packs. Mia and I claimed a small section of the clearing, leaving the better seating for our guests without even discussing it. We opened our packs, where we'd put lunch fixings on top, bulky, fresh sandwiches I'd pulled from the fridge this morning and that were the last gasp of civilization for the next week. Most of them were thick-sliced, oven roasted turkey I'd brined and cooked myself before layering with Havarti cheese, cranberry jelly, and baby spinach, but I also had two caprese on ciabatta for the vegetarians in the group and a hummus sandwich bursting with fresh vegetables I'd made for Mia almost despite myself. I'd freeze-dried a bunch of that hummus for later in the week, but the vegetables were another story.

"Here." I handed it to her.

She unwrapped a corner of the paper it was in and peeked inside. "You didn't have to."

"You said it yourself: we're all in this together."

"At least for now."

Before I could dig into what she meant by that, someone said, "Holy shit," though it was muffled by a mouthful of sandwich. "This is amazing."

The corner of Mia's mouth quirked up. "Your adoring public awaits."

I glanced around at our campers and smiled. "Now, don't get too used to it. Things will turn more rustic after this."

Mia said, "But no less delicious, and not just because food tastes better after hiking all day. All right, T and I know something about all of you from your intake forms and other pre-trip communication, but let's make sure we get properly acquainted. T already asked about your favorite food on our extensive questionnaire, so let's go around, introduce yourself, and tell us all something we don't know." She hummed, her face twisting up in mock contemplation. "Something like…where you were born and where you live now, which are both boring, so also tell us what you spend most of your time doing outside working and sleeping and what you wish you could spend most of your time doing. Let's start with you, Laura," she said to the woman on her left.

Mia pulled off a big bite of her sandwich while Laura talked, and it took everything in me not to watch her eat. I unwrapped my own lunch and dug in, listening to everyone fumble through being put on the spot, admitting to *Real-Housewives*-type vices and to not living the lives they wished they did. Four friends, three straight couples, and two sisters were in the group. Generally, the more people I met, the more I knew we were all pretty much the same. It took a lot to actually separate yourself from the crowd, not that doing so was even a great idea. Then there was Mia, unknowably different in my mind.

I'd managed to nod and eat my way through all dozen of our campers' introductions, retaining some information but not nearly enough, and I still managed to be completely unprepared when we got to me. "I'm T. I was born in Charlotte and still live there, though I spent some years in Asheville before going back to school." I always said that, *school*, since it neatly hid my lack of a formal degree. "When I'm not cooking, I'm generally eating…or drinking tea, hence my nickname. If I had my way, I'd…well, cook," I laughed along with everyone else, "but in my own restaurant, not that preparing food for you all as a camp chef isn't one of the best things ever." It was a stock answer, and I tried not to think if it were actually true.

Mia was watching me, which made me self-conscious. "Thanks for feeding us, T," she said, which set off a chorus of murmured agreement. She took a bite of her sandwich and seemed not at all inclined to answer her own questions.

"Mia actually grew up just a couple miles from me and is the oldest sister of our usual guide, Lucia. Where do you live now?"

She glanced at her compass and pointed into the woods. "About forty or fifty miles that way, at least some of the year."

"And…?" I prompted.

"I read a lot and take care of my cabin. I used to dream about being a wildlife illustrator, so I guess I'd spend more time drawing if I could. As long as it didn't cut into my hiking or hammock time, that is," she said with a wide smile that raised that dimple. My kryptonite.

I hadn't known that about the illustrator aspirations, and I wanted to dig into it more, but Mia got up, her knees making a faint crackling sound, and passed around a trash sack for everyone's sandwich papers and whatever wrappers they produced from their pockets and packs. Everything we brought in had to get carried out. She said, "If you've been drinking enough, you should have to pee, so we'll hang here until everyone takes care of business before starting out again so we can have plenty of time to relax at camp before T fixes us something fabulous for dinner."

No pressure or anything.

The afternoon was much like the morning, which I found comforting about hiking. Sensory input changed and stretched, turning long tracks of trail into a blur of one background or another: forest or meadow or windy, bare bald. But then that landscape would be made unique by the arrival of an interesting animal, the glance of a deer, or momentary fright of a black snake curled in a patch of sunshine. I failed at not thinking about Mia, connecting the sketching she'd done on my couch with what she'd produced in a similar notebook sometimes when I'd come over to hang out with Lucia. But she'd gone to UNC Asheville for business, a weird fact that had stuck in my mind despite the years. Could drawing and business be farther away from each other? We were all small worlds of contradiction.

For a while, partly to distract myself from feckless pondering about Mia's internal multitudes, I fell into a soft conversation with one of the sisters, Melody, who confided that she was dragging her kin away from all her many screens as a low-key intervention. Neither of them had camping experience and were wearing two of the four rental packs Mia had assembled, but they'd whiled away plenty of hours in a backyard treehouse as girls. Now, though, it seemed that they couldn't have a simple conversation without Stephanie's nose being buried in her phone.

Melody looked to where her sister was walking a few people ahead of us. "I think Steph is okay when she's moving, but I worry about nights at camp. Hell, I worry about nights at camp for me, too. I'm not used to entertaining myself anymore."

"Don't worry about it. If you're also not used to hiking this much, you'll be pretty zonked out. After dinner, staring into the fire is often enough to keep people occupied, but Mia and I have plenty of activities we can trot out in case of a mutiny. I wasn't kidding about the ghost stories."

"Mia's so knowledgeable. And beautiful! Her skin is flawless. You grew up with her?" Melody waved her hand in front of her face while we passed through a cloud of small insects. If there was one thing I disliked about hiking, it was bugs, especially on a muggy summer day, which would be on us soon enough.

"She's six years older, so 'with' is a stretch, but she'd sometimes let Lucia and me tag along with her on adventures. You and Steph seem pretty close."

As I'd hoped, that got her talking about her sister, her voice dropped even lower so Steph wouldn't overhear from where she plodded along in the middle of the group, which had gotten strung out enough that I only rarely caught glimpses of Mia up front, and not her flawless skin. Melody should've seen Mia in her bright blue high school graduation gown that Lucia and I had accidentally burned up in one astounding flash after Mia had disrobed for the day. It wasn't the first or last time I'd done something like that with an open flame, but I'd vowed to be careful about cheap polyester from then on.

While everyone else flopped down when we reached our campsite after the hike, Mia and I got busy. We helped everyone set up their tents, pointed out areas to use as our latrine, debated the "community" lean-to and decided against it, given the weather forecast, and gathered wood for the cook and camp fires. Mia set her lips in a firm line and used a small hatchet to break up larger fallen branches, toned arm swinging down, the hatchet head meeting wood with solid thunks and sending splinters flying. Her breath was audible through her nose, and the impact reverberated across her flesh. Unlike Lucia, she didn't let me spell her, telling me to work on my cook fire with what we'd already gathered.

I could make a fire in my sleep, even without matches. It was all about kindling and air and, of course, that first spark. All living things needed oxygen, and fire was no exception. Kindling had to be arranged to allow the movement of that portion of fire's fuel across the flames; usually this was either in a "teepee" or "log-cabin" configuration around a center of highly-combustible material—either paper or wood shavings. Then it came down to patience, making sure the fire was established before trying to make it larger and more self-sustaining. Then, for the cook fire, spits or racks or buried areas had to be planned so that I could do everything I needed to without having to reshape a fire that very much didn't want to be moved.

Cooking for fourteen people in a full kitchen was something I could do on autopilot, balancing bake durations and available burners so that everything turned out at just the right time, piping hot and ready for family-style serving. Here I had one fire—maybe two if I insinuated myself into the one meant for gathering around and enjoying (and occasional s'mores roasting)—and much less than my entire cookware set. I thanked the gods and technology for the lighter weight, blue steel, flat-bottomed pan I used on the trail instead of my trusty but heavy cast iron. I could make things easier on myself by assembling all our meals in advance and freeze-drying them that way, which would only require some water and time before serving, but part of gourmet camp cooking was, well, actually cooking. Seeing food prepared was as much a flavor enhancement as MSG, al-fresco dining, physical exhaustion, and deep hunger.

Who could resist the sizzle of fajitas? No one, that's who. I pulled bags of freeze-dried ingredients from my pack, which I'd stuffed as strategically as possible so I wouldn't have to dump everything out all the time. Marinated chicken, refried beans, sliced peppers and onions and carrots, a sack of quick-cooking rice, my herbs and spices, and my mainstay grapeseed oil, which could take higher temperatures without scorching and provided the heavy dash of fat we all needed on the trail.

But first, tortillas. I poured some warm water from my pan into the bag of corn flour and salt I'd premixed and let it set. It was ludicrous to make tortillas on the trail, especially for this big of a group, since I had to finish with at least thirty, but I'd practiced at home and could fit three in my pan at a time, which sped the process along. Before long, I was in the rhythm of rolling out balls of dough into flat rounds between the flexible cutting board I had on the ground and the small propane canister I carried in case of such wet weather that I couldn't get a fire going. I'd roll out three while cooking and flipping another three in the skillet, lifting the skillet off the fire whenever it threatened to get too hot. I was left with two stacks of soft, warm tortillas I kept toasty in foil packets I tucked in close to the fire. I was never more serious or more joyful than when I was cooking around a fire.

I was so intent on my task I didn't notice my audience until I straightened up to stretch my back. "Hey." I smiled. "Dinner'll be ready in twenty minutes. Mia's got sanitizer and some extra plates and utensils for those of you who forgot yours or told us you didn't have any." I took a sip from my Misfitters branded camp mug, my trusty and stained tea diffuser resting on its upturned lid next to it. "You're welcome to hang around here with me, but now that Mia's got the main campfire going, you'll probably be more comfortable there."

Mia wandered over, brushing her hands on her hiking pants. "Absolutely, pull up a rock or your camp stool or a sleeping pad if you want, but I know I find it pretty entertaining to watch T do her thing. And drink her tea while she does it."

I studied her, wondering how much of this was an act. I wanted too much to believe it was true, but the change in Mia from even this morning made me distrust everything. I reminded myself I had better and more important things to think about than what Mia did or didn't think of me. "Sure, you're welcome to hang around here, but don't get too close, and no swiping food off the pan; that's the chef's privilege only."

I was left with Melody, Steph, and the mixed couple who'd been chattering earlier on the trail, the husband of one and wife of another. I wondered where their spouses were but didn't have time to worry too much about it. The guy, David, seemed to be a bit of a survivalist and questioned me about the freeze-drying process to a degree butting up against annoying. He monopolized the conversation, though the woman, Sandy, managed a question or two about my favorite teas. I suspected Melody was hanging around to keep Steph occupied during her screen detox, which was fine with me. Cooking took some amount of concentration, but I was never one to turn my back on company.

After I'd measured out hot water and poured it into the bag of freeze-dried yellow rice so it could reconstitute to its fluffy original state, I theatrically held up the large bag of rehydrated vegetables over the hot pan, and they all fell quiet. I dropped in the mound of vegetables in the shimmering oil and sprinkled the popping, sizzling mound with dried Mexican oregano and a shower of salt. After a minute, I wrapped my overshirt from early in the day around the pan's long handle and shook and flicked my wrist, sending veggies sliding and flipping over to get coated in oil and spices and start cooking evenly. My audience applauded, and I couldn't suppress a grin.

With a separate pan of hot water, I warmed my tea and rehydrated the refried beans, massaging the mix in the bag I'd packed them in. Before adding the chicken to the hot pan, I scooped out three servings of the vegetables for the vegetarians and Mia and set them aside. While the chicken cooked, making my own mouth water and giving that wonderful sizzle we all craved, I carefully rehydrated my two bags of salsa with cool water, one mild and one hot, and started handing out tortillas.

As the night progressed, conversation and energy ebbing and flowing, campers drifting away from the fire and back in changed clothes or wearing a fleece, Mia got quieter, and I filled in the gaps when it looked like people were getting bored. I watched her through the flickering flames, the firelight casting changing shadows on her face, which looked...static. Not thoughtful or tired or pissed but kind of checked out. Of course what did I know? It was dark, and she might have just been lost staring into the fire. I didn't know her at all, I reminded myself, and I was never going to. She was here to save us this season before vanishing again, probably permanently.

The yawning started early, though I was still wide awake. It was always this way the first trip. I was jazzed and nervous, reviewing what I'd packed and the possible mistakes I'd made. I couldn't keep myself from iterating through all the different ways things could go wrong or thinking ahead to tomorrow and what I'd have to do while Mia took the group on a long day hike to a beautiful waterfall I never got to see on these trips because I was busy at camp. This was the best kind of work, but it was still work.

Before long, Mia and I were the only ones around the fire, anchoring down opposite sides of the circle. She'd done a beautiful job with it, laying out stones and logs to provide the right draft and venting to keep smoke from getting in anyone's eyes. I geared up to compliment her on her handiwork or talk about how much lighter our packs were going to be on the trek to the next campsite or, more likely, say something stupid and irrelevant before crawling into my own sleeping bag and pretending she wasn't dozing off just a few feet away. But before I could, I heard something back around the tents.

It was probably nothing. Or, you know, it could be a black bear, enticed by the bits of leftover food I hadn't yet secured. I glanced over in the general direction of the sound but saw nothing. I didn't often get the heebie-jeebies in the woods, but I was admittedly on edge with Mia lurking there, quiet and withdrawn—but now looking at the tents as well. Then I heard it again, loud and long enough to recognize it: sex. I laughed and saw that Mia was smiling now.

"Not a bear," I said.

"Not unless that bear is getting busy."

We listened for a while. "They have way too much energy after this day."

"We shouldn't be doing this," she said.

"Well, don't you have to be a bit of an exhibitionist to have such vigorous sex in a tent with other people around?"

Mia took her water bottle and moved next to me. "They may be exhibitionists, but I'm not a voyeur, so...should we talk about tomorrow?"

"I think we should talk about who's having the sex." It wasn't immature to say this when we were talking about something so brazen.

"It's Nick and Heidi."

"You know, you used to be fun."

"I used to be a lot of things," she said to the fire, frowning a little.

"Nick and Heidi, huh?"

"We have three couples, and they're the only ones who hung with each other all day."

"Huh. Is that how couples behave? It's been so long for me I can't remember."

She shifted a little, folding one leg under the other, a loosened hiking boot flopping over to the side. "I find that hard to believe."

"I know, right? I'm a total catch. I hibernate during the winter and play with fire in the woods all summer. Who wouldn't want to date me?" It was so much easier to talk to people when you were both focused on a campfire and not each other. Probably too easy.

"You want to open your own restaurant?"

I laughed, waving that off. "Me and about a million other chefs, so I'm not holding my breath. You want to get paid to draw wildlife?"

After a beat, she said, "I've learned to be very careful about what I let myself want."

She didn't seem inclined to say anything else, and I took a sip of my cooling tea in our conversational lull. While we faded, Nick and Heidi took things up to the next—and final—level. I think they may have tried to be quiet, but it didn't work. I smiled and felt a pang of jealousy. I had dated someone briefly before the holidays, but it hadn't gone anywhere, just a month of irregular sex that had barely blunted my accumulated appetite.

Though Mia was sitting next to me, she seemed far away again and unapproachable. It was time for us to call it a night, though I still wasn't sleepy and would surely stare at the very dark ceiling of my tent for an hour before drifting off. She shifted again, and in a sudden panic at the thought that she was going to leave me here, I said, "You were good with everyone today. Different."

"Friendly, you mean."

I shrugged.

"I can play a role well when I have to. I've had tons of practice."

When she didn't say any more, I expended all sorts of effort to repress the dramatic sigh just dying to be let loose into the night air. "You do that a lot, you know, say this thing that should be the start of something but that you make into the end."

"Believe me, T. You don't want to know." Now she did get up, unfolding herself and running a hand through her hair. "Thanks for dinner. It was delicious. I'm not sure how I'm going to go back to my regular food after this summer."

"Nuts and seeds and berries?" I asked in a vain attempt to hold her here with me.

"You got it."

I waited by the fire while she disappeared to our latrine area, came back, and zipped herself into her tent. I lay on the ground, resting my head on my hands. It was going to be a long night.

CHAPTER SIX

Days on the trail were all similar to each other and long. I cooked or hiked or set up and broke down tents. I gathered kindling and wood and raised rivers of sweat swinging the hatchet or hovering over my cook fire. Each trip was a string of getting up early to make breakfast and staying up late to entertain and pack up after dinner and dessert. Steph and Melody became my sous chefs, Melody clearly trying to keep Steph from going out of her mind without her devices and a high-speed, fiberoptic conduit to the outside world.

Somehow the work felt even harder with Mia being infallibly upbeat and serenely positive, perfectly playing the role of gracious host and guide. The longer she inhabited this character of hers, the more foreign she got to me. We didn't repeat the fireside conversation of the first night, partly because I hid in my tent, not wanting to see her become herself, remote in a way more wrenching than when she was "playing at" being Lucia's substitute. At the same time, sex was on my mind constantly after overhearing Nick and Heidi. It wasn't as if that was the first time I'd been uncomfortably aware of some campers going at it, but it had set up a deep ache in me that no amount of work could dislodge. Mia found it hard to believe that I was monumentally single? Did that mean she would date me if she weren't the original woman of mystery? The idea was ludicrous, but it haunted me in the still air of my tent when I should've been sleeping.

I watched her too much, caught on the way she moved and the smiles she gave to everyone but me—or only to me when other people were looking. She was lithe and strong and had a quiet capability that affected me deeply. Everything she did was sure and right, from the way she pounded a tent stake to how she squatted on the trail to point out something to our campers, whether an animal track or a particular plant that could help you stay alive if you got lost in the woods, which a frankly ridiculous number of people did every year.

At night, it was impossible not to think about her in the next tent over, tucked into her sleeping bag against the evening chill, her body both soft and strong. But then, in the morning, she'd be either deeply silent or the social version of herself, neither of which I could reconcile with my memories or the quiet moments we'd had together since she'd appeared back in my life. One morning, she was up even before me, sitting outside her tent, bent over a pad of paper, her hair obscuring what she was sketching, inscrutable in every way.

After our lunch break on the third day, it started to rain. We'd known it was a distinct possibility but had been walking under deep canopy and hadn't seen it coming. The trees caught a lot of the rain when it started, and we took that momentary reprieve to draw up as a group, everyone digging through their gear for pack covers and jackets. There was grumbling all around, but it was relatively good-natured, some people foregoing jackets in the stated hope that the rain would wash the worst of their own smell off them and their clothes. It was warm enough that no one would be in danger of hypothermia, but there were better ways to get clean. Mia and I gathered off to the side and made a game plan.

I said, "If I hurry, I can get the main shelter up and stockpile wood so it can dry out, assuming you think the rain's going to be with us for a while."

She grimaced. "It could be here all the way through tomorrow. What are the chances of a fire?"

"I'll pick up dry stuff as I go along and tuck them under my pack cover. It might be a little smoky, but we can definitely get something started. If I can hustle and pull as much wood as I can carry under the shelter tonight, that'll help for tomorrow. Depending on what I find, I'll tuck some inside my tent with me."

"Lucky wood," she said, the words almost lost in the patter of rain in the canopy. "Sounds like a plan. I guess you should get going, huh?"

But I was stuck on that offhand comment and couldn't quite move—at least until a fat raindrop hit me squarely on the nose, which made my face scrunch up and Mia laugh. I glanced up at the sky. "Okay. I can take a hint. Catch you later," I said to Mia and took off at a trot up the trail, my bag bouncing and shifting until I tightened up my straps enough for it to sit against me more snugly than usual. I did a jog/walk routine for the next four miles, putting as much distance between me and the group as I could—or at least put distance between me and Mia. Did she even know she'd said that? Did she know how much her laugh affected me, despite my best efforts to be chill? Every time I slowed down a little to catch my breath, her smile came back to me along with the idea of her being jealous of firewood next to me in my tent, and I sped up to dispel them both. Don't go there. Focus on the basics: shelter, fire, and food.

By the time I got to the campsite, the rain cover over my pack was stretched tight over mostly dry kindling, and I was a hot, sweaty mess under my jacket. The rain felt downright refreshing in its coolness, and I stripped to my sports bra to get to work. First, my tent, which was easily accessible in my pack and set up in a few minutes, including its rain fly. I dragged my pack inside and squatted next to it, digging around for the rest of what I needed, rain dripping from my hair into its open zipper. I had to pull out half of our food and my cookware to get at what I was looking for: the tarp and poles Lucia and I had fashioned together into something we could use as a community lean-to in just these situations. It was really a two-person job to get it up, but I struggled through it, swearing the whole time and getting thwapped right across the face with one of the tent poles when I tried to make it do something it didn't want to.

The group still hadn't arrived by then, so I went scouting for wood, finding some mostly-dry pieces under thickly leaved trees and hurrying them back under my makeshift shelter, where I broke them down with the hatchet Mia had handed over to me before my mad dash over here. With half of the kindling I'd protected on the way and a couple of matches from my waterproof safe, I got a small fire started, next to which I piled wood that I broke down, hoping to warm some of the moisture out of the pieces over time. Knowing that at least I was going to be stuck here all day tomorrow and that some of the campers would decline the opportunity for a day hike in the rain, we were going to need a bunch more wood to keep the fire going. I gathered and cut down and gathered and cut down until I about wanted to die from it.

I was taking a break outside the shelter to let the rain rinse some of the sweat off me and have a much-needed drink when Mia stepped into the clearing and stopped. She was staring at me. No, not just staring. Even through the diffuse curtain of rain, I could tell she was devouring me with her gaze. I felt conflicting desires to stand there and let her or remember where I'd left my shirt and cover up, but before I could decide on a course of action, other campers filed in around Mia, and I heard a wolf whistle.

"Who knew our camp chef was so sexy?"

"She can cook and is a hottie, too?"

"What a catch!"

I laughed and struck a mock bodybuilder pose, pretending to flex muscles I didn't actually have—or had but were camouflaged by the padding that was a byproduct of my passion for food. Hiking kept it mostly in check, but it was still early in the season.

"Welcome home! Mia and I will help you set up your tents, and don't forget to use your handy quick-dry Misfitters camp towels when you change out of your soggy clothes. I'll put water on for tea or coffee, and I just might have some hot chocolate available if you all ask nicely—or keep complimenting me that way."

I found my shirt and ducked into it and let myself get carried into the flurry of activity to settle everyone in before starting on meal prep. With one fire and the close confines of the lean-to, tonight's dinner would be nothing fancy, but it needed to be warm and filling. Mostly I tried to forget how Mia had looked at me—and how I'd responded to that look: yes, drizzle me with honey and consume me. It had sent a shiver down my spine and heat flooding my chest, and I was so thankful for that wolf whistle and half-joking comments about my physique for helping to dispel my arousal. I tried not to glance Mia's way and let us divide the work so we were both busy but not collaborating together on anything. Still, I heard her voice, cheerful and joking, trying to keep anyone from getting too down about the weather and their soggy socks and boots.

Most people were in their tents when I got to the lean-to with bags of tea, coffee, and cocoa and a pot of water I'd probably have to fill and boil a few times to be able to satisfy everyone's hot-drink cravings. I hadn't yet dried off, though given the growing coolness in the air and my dwindling physical activity, I would have to get around to it soon. My shirt was suctioned to my chest and stomach, and I was trying to separate it from my skin when Mia came around the bend with an armload of wood.

She stopped just inside the shelter. "Oh."

"Hey." I squeezed the hem of my shirt, sending a spattering of water onto the mostly dry ground near the fire. I glanced down at the wrinkled bunch of fabric. "This is a losing battle, huh?"

"You were probably better off not wearing it at all."

Especially if it made her look at me in the way she had. We both gravitated toward the fire, partly for the warmth of it and partly because of some force I couldn't identify or resist. "Maybe if I were the only one here."

"That's the benefit of living like a hermit. No witnesses."

"I mean, who doesn't like twirling around naked in the rain, but don't you get lonely?" I held my breath at this brazen question.

Her arms tightened around the wood she held. "Desperately."

I was caught in her gaze, still not quite breathing. "Mia. What happened back then?"

Which, of course, was the wrong thing to say. Her face melted down into a frown, and she glanced away. "Nothing. Everything. It doesn't matter, and you really don't want to know. Do you want this wood here or in your tent with you?"

Even though I'd been telling *myself* over and over that I didn't want to know, I had to rein in my natural pissy response to her words. "Whatever works for you. You know best." Okay, so some slipped out anyway.

She dropped the wood on a pre-existing pile. "That's not what I mean. The whole thing is such a long, tired story. I'm glad you were too young to know what was going on, and I'd like to keep it that way."

"I'm not a little sister you need to protect, and Lucia knows everything, right?"

"Lucia *thinks* she knows everything."

"I'm not just Lucia's dumb friend anymore."

She took a small step closer. "I never thought you were a dumb friend."

"Then why won't you tell me anything?"

Her answer was an explosion of broad gesticulation and emotion only slightly tempered by the drum of rain on the tarp above us. "Because I don't want anyone to know that stuff about me, especially you!" She disappeared back into the rain, but before I could decide whether or not to follow her, Melody and Steph ducked in under the tarp, mostly dry in their evening camp clothes, soft pants and long-sleeved T-shirts, each with a different college on them.

Melody said, "Wow, you haven't changed yet?"

I laughed, dismayed that even I could hear the bitter edge to it. "This isn't a secure your own mask before helping others situation." I glanced down at the battered pot full of water that was being licked at by orange and yellow flames, not to mention a healthy dose of light gray smoke from the wet wood. "Water's just about ready. What's your pleasure?"

Steph said, "Did I hear you mention hot chocolate?"

I grinned. "I did, indeed. Straight up or spicy?"

"Spicy sounds heavenly."

"Melody?" I asked.

"I'm just here for the fire."

I let myself get distracted by preparing Steph's drink while the two sisters settled in next to the fire after checking which way the breeze was blowing to stay out of the smoke. Mia hadn't gotten around to working her magic with rocks and logs around the fire. I felt a pang both wistful and angry but squashed it while adding the final dash of cinnamon to Steph's hot chocolate and handing it over.

"How's the tech detox going?"

"Oh, Melody told you about that, huh?" she said and gave her sister a stink eye I suspected Melody had endured since childhood.

"I'm lucky I've never spent much time in front of a screen, so I haven't gotten sucked into it."

She blew across the top of her mug, sending steam scattering. Her hands were folded tight around it. "I guess kicking heroin is worse, but I wouldn't bet on it. Don't you go crazy out here not knowing what's happening in the world?"

I pulled my shirt away from its clingwrap position against my front. "Not really. Maybe that's selfish, but most of what's going on either doesn't matter to me or isn't something I have the ability to change in any significant way. I'd rather tune into the woods or the smell and feel of a perfectly ripe heirloom tomato."

They stared at me.

"That sounds naïve, I know. I pay attention to the news leading up to elections and always vote, but I don't have the thing in me that allows obsession about 'the world,'" I put the phrase in finger quotes that made me feel self-conscious. The drowned rat expounding on some half-assed Zen way to live. Mia was the hermit, not me.

"Well, then, you're healthier than all of us," Steph said before taking a sip of her chocolate and groaning. "Good God, what did you put in this?"

"This, that, and a little of the other." My standard answer.

"I wholeheartedly approve of you shutting out the world if it helps you concoct stuff like this." She shoved the mug at Melody's mouth. "Try it."

Melody made a face at Steph's insistence but took a sip and smiled. "Delicious."

Steph said, "Who knew I'd eat some of the best food I've had in the last couple years in the middle of friggin nowhere."

"I think we should let T get dried off, don't you? She's still drenched."

"It's okay, really. I'll wait and see if anyone wants some of this hot water now that it's made. And Steph, I've heard that there's something that happens to the brain when you surround yourself in green spaces and eliminate screens, but it takes three days, I think? Or maybe it's a week? Anyway, I'm sure you'll be over the worst of it soon."

"Now if we can only keep her from relapsing when we get back to civilization."

"Don't hold your breath," Steph said, but she took another sip of her cocoa and smiled.

It was a cozy evening around the fire with everyone chowing down on my Massaman curry and rice (chickpeas for the vegetarians and Mia and beef for everyone else). The tents around us were festooned with clothes people wanted the rain to wash the stink out of before taking them inside to hopefully dry before having to wear them again. The rain was steady but not torrential, and a calm breeze meant we were mostly safe from spray under the lean-to. About half the campers had stories of epically rainy hiking trips or family vacations, and dinner was accompanied by a stream of growing exaggerations about the depth of floods or the size of toxic-mold blooms.

Everyone seemed to be having a decent time despite (or maybe even because of) the weather except Mia, who sat as far away from me as she could and shirked her number-one-hostess persona to stare into the fire. She even left half of her dinner uneaten and cooling on her plate until Nick asked if she were going to finish it, evidently needing to keep up his strength for the sex he and Heidi were going to have that night, again. I wasn't one to begrudge anyone a good time in the sack but hearing them go at it would be like fingernails on a chalkboard after that aborted conversation with Mia. Maybe the rain would drown it out.

Speaking of rain, Mia had her palm-sized weather radio to her ear, and I tried to predict the forecast myself based on the changes in her expression. She finally shut it off and, after waiting for a lull in the conversation, said, "Good news and bad news. The weather system is moving a little faster than predicted, but the rain's going to be with us at least until tomorrow afternoon. I'm still planning on a day hike from here for anyone interested in heading up one of the tributaries into some pretty interesting geological formations. It's a little too long to try to wait until the rain passes, but maybe we'll catch a dry second half. Otherwise, you can stay at camp with T and try to keep from getting too stir crazy."

The group dickered around a little bit, dividing into stay and go factions but without any friction—although the folks staying were picked on in a good-natured way for being wusses. Mia got up and stretched through it, tucking the radio into her pocket and seeming to keep an informal running tally of who she might have with her on an adventure in the morning. She made excuses of tiredness and being stuffed by my dinner and trotted off into the rain toward her tent.

I mumbled something about being right back to the folks sitting close to me, who clearly didn't care, and dashed after Mia, catching up to her just as she ducked into the rainfly of her tent. I crowded in after her, causing some cursing and grunting from us both until I was curled up in a squat mostly outside her tent but still inside the rainfly, and she was pushed back onto the roll of her sleeping bag and pad.

"What the hell, T," she finally said when we were still again. "Zip the fly or you'll get everything wet."

"Or wetter than it already is?" I said, but I was already zipping us in together. "We need to talk."

She closed her eyes. "Do we really? The world is full of so much talking, and I don't think it's the better for it."

"I can't keep doing this."

"Lucia was always a bit of a drama queen, but she really rubbed off on you, didn't she?"

Now I was angry, which overrode my ever-present hesitancy and made me say, "I don't know which person is real: the warm guide who reminds me so much of Lucia's older, kick-ass sister, or this...this...*this*," I motioned at her crouched form.

"No one is just a single thing."

"I *know* that."

"Then grow up and start acting like it. I never asked you to figure me out. I never asked you to get under my skin. I didn't ask for any of this, Harper." And then she grabbed the back of my neck, pulled me close, and kissed me.

It was rough, too hard and angry for me to feel the fullness of her lips or register much of anything at all besides her aching closeness and the squeeze of her fingers against my damp hair and flesh. I wanted to tell her to wait, to stop, to at least slow down and let me participate, but instead of any of that, I pushed against her, toppling us both onto the lumps of her gear and one insistent tree root I found with my knee.

She opened her mouth to my tongue, and I felt the heat of her breath against my cheek like our kiss had knocked the wind out of her. She wasn't the only one, since my heart was beating with such a racket that it took up my whole chest, making air a faint memory. Mia was firm and solid against me, her hand still pulling against my neck even though we were as flush together as we could get around her pack and bag and the opening of her tent, through which my legs still stretched.

God, I was kissing Mia Renata Mary Guzman, and she was kissing me back with a fierce intensity, making soft noises that sounded like a cross between moaning and pleading. She tasted like curry and smelled like woodsmoke, and her skin scorched where it touched mine despite the dampness of rain. We twisted and moved, making room in the cramped nylon confines, blindly shifting gear and each other until she pushed hard against me, and I ended up on my back, that tree root digging into my ass now, not that I cared one bit with Mia angled shallowly above me, resting on one elbow, holding herself up with her other arm.

When she opened her eyes, I couldn't distinguish pupil from chocolate iris in the dimness of the tent, which was just barely lit by the campfire. There was light enough to see that she was shaking her head in a narrow back and forth, and her eyebrows were drawn together, making a canyon of that crease in between. "Harper," she said.

For the first time in years, I loved hearing that name, my real one. I reached up to brush a heavy lock of hair back behind one of her ears. "Kiss me again."

She blinked slowly and hovered there, not moving, our legs intertwined. Then she groaned and erased the distance between us. Our kiss was slow this time, and deep. I wanted to swallow her whole like an exotic delicacy, drink her like champagne. Delicious, I thought. Delicious. The insistent press of that tree root only enhanced her sweetness, a sour note in a perfectly-balanced dish. I grabbed a fistful of her shirt and tangled my fingers in a belt loop to stay totally here with her.

Then her mouth pulled a breath away, and she ground her forehead into mine. "Shit," she whispered and sat up. "Shit," she repeated a few more times for good measure and shifted as far away from me as she could get in the tent, which thankfully wasn't that far. She turned on her headlamp that was on her sleeping bag so we could see each other.

"No," I said. "Don't."

"I promised myself I wouldn't."

"Wouldn't what? Drive me crazy, then kiss me like I was the first drink of water you've had for days?"

She reached out to me but reversed course halfway there and crossed her arms. "I can't get involved."

"Why not?"

"I just can't."

I pressed the heel of a hand against the center of my chest. "This is what I'm talking about. Or was talking about before you did…what you just did. You act one way and then another and give answers that only raise more questions."

"That's because there aren't any good answers, T." The words had a snap to them, and my nickname increased the gap between us, which I hated.

"I'm not asking for good answers. I'm asking for something real."

She laughed. "Believe me. You don't want my reality. I'm sorry, I really am. If you hadn't followed me in here, I would've been okay. I could've kept my distance."

"I just wanted to talk," I said, but she looked at me with one raised eyebrow. "I assumed we would just talk, okay? Get things straight between us. I mean, I've wanted to kiss you for ages, probably since I was a preteen and didn't know what I was feeling, but that was the last thing on my mind when I came after you." I watched her, trying to see beyond her frown to what she was thinking. "Talk to me, Mia."

She nodded her head toward the campfire. "We have work to do."

"Really?"

She took one of my hands in both of hers and massaged my palm and the muscle at the base of my thumb, sending warmth all the way up my arm. "I made a mistake. I'd take it back if I could."

"You would?"

"No." Her laugh was sharp and surprised sounding. "You were a cute kid, but now you're grown up in the best way. If you were someone else, and we were somewhere else, but we're not, and I'm…" She shrugged.

"Something you're not going to tell me."

She let go of my hand. "Believe me, T, you don't want to know." Then, even though she was the one who had left the lean-to for this tent, she donned her headlamp, unzipped the rainfly, and stepped outside.

I lay back against her sleeping bag. I could still feel her fingers on mine and her breath against my cheek. We wanted each other, but she wouldn't let herself have me the way she most definitely could. I wished I could talk to Lucia, who usually helped me unpack my many failures with women (or, more frequently, listened to me lament during dry spells), but I couldn't imagine that would go down the way I hoped. At this point, I wasn't sure what Lucia knew about Mia and what Mia had successfully hidden from everyone. Besides, they were sisters. Besides, Mia was ex-communicated from the Guzmans. Besides, I was supposed to be keeping my eye on The Misfitters' ball, not Mia's arms when she was chopping wood.

I couldn't talk to Lucia, forget about Venus, and I couldn't screw this up, all of which was probably a lot like what Mia was feeling. That kiss had been mind-altering, and I ached to feel her weight against me again, but Mia was right in her wrongness. We were us, and we were here, and that meant we had work to do and had to keep it professional—or as professional as The Misfitters ever did, given how personal the job was to all of us.

CHAPTER SEVEN

I was up at the crack of dawn, fishing for trout to cook for dinner in a misty drizzle. I stood on a bank of the large creek swollen from the night's rain and cast out my line, my hat shielding my face from most of the rain, water dripping from the elbows and hem of my jacket. I liked fishing—not only the end result of crispy, herbed trout, fresh and hot from my pan but the meditative process of it. Lucia got bored with it quickly, and Venus was incapable of catching anything without a net practically as big as she was, but I could spend hours walking along a bank or wading up to my thighs in quickly running water to catch whatever was biting.

I'd spent most of the night listening to the rain and trying not to think of being in Mia's tent with her, her hand on my neck, her tongue in my mouth. It was a losing battle, and I'd been downright thrilled when dawn broke through the cloud cover, making it just bright enough for me not to hook myself on a lure or trip headfirst into the creek in the darkness. As miserable as getting soaked to the bone could be, rain was usually a soporific, and I wasn't surprised that I had at least an hour to myself before I heard the first zip of a tent and wet, stumbling steps through the trees to our latrine area.

I was going to have to stop what I was doing pretty soon to get a fire started for hot drinks and breakfast, which would be oatmeal today for sure, given the continued rain. But before then, I cast my line again, hoping to add one more fish to the growing collection in the mesh bag I had submerged in the creek, held in place on the bank by a large rock. I would eat trout first thing in the morning in a heartbeat, but while breakfast for dinner was an accepted thing, the reverse didn't hold true for most people.

My line twitched, and I waited for another nibble before jerking my pole and hopefully setting my hook in the fish's mouth, something I wondered if Mia would consider barbaric. Whether she would or not, my line played out as the fish swam downstream, and I started to reel it in, pulling back and taking up the slack in a short, easy rhythm. I saw the fish ripple just beneath the surface about ten feet away when I felt someone next to me and said, "Just a sec. I'm almost done here and then I'll get the fire started."

"I was just saying hi." I knew Mia's voice even before I glanced around and saw her, her eyes darker than usual and bruised looking.

I almost lost the grip on my rod. "Oh, hey. Sorry, I'm doing carnivore things."

"Don't worry about it. I'll take care of the fire and put some water on if you want to keep going. You deserve a meal off."

I continued to reel in the fish, not wanting it to slip the hook and get away. "I don't get meals off until November, but I'd appreciate you starting the fire. There's kindling and some wood in my tent if the stuff under the lean-to is too wet."

"Okay," she said, but I didn't hear her leave.

The fish was close now, and I grabbed the line to pull it out of the water. Trout number five, maybe ten inches long. I let my rod drop, laid the fish on the ground, and hit it hard with the butt of my knife as quickly as I could to stun it unconscious.

I pulled out the hook in one swift move and cut into its gills before taking it back to the creek for it to bleed out. It probably looked cruel and heartless from a vegan perspective, but it was the most humane way I knew of killing what I caught.

I jumped when Mia started talking. "Do you remember when I took you and Lucia fishing off the bridge that summer you were both twelve?"

Of course I remembered. Any time Mia let us tag along with her had been an event to my awestruck, awkward, younger self. I answered with a nod.

"You literally shrieked when you tried to take that bluegill off your hook."

It had been jumping in my hand, trying to make a great escape, and I'd been afraid to squeeze it too hard. "Lucia was ruthless. She gutted them almost before you pulled them out of the water."

"She was a tough kid."

"Hey, I was tough, too."

"Still are," she said. "Just in a different way. About last night—"

"No, you're right. There's too much talking in the world today. We're supposed to be focusing on our campers and, you know," I motioned around me, "nature and shit."

"Nature and shit is good." She glanced at the cluster of tents, which remained still and peaceful looking. "We might have another half hour before a critical mass of people emerge. Mind if I have a go?" She indicated the fishing pole that was still lying on the ground next to me.

"Doesn't that conflict with your veganism?"

"Yes and no. You're going to catch more, anyway, and you clearly know what you're doing to minimize their suffering. They're not going to go to waste, and I'm sure you'll honor them well in your frying pan. My being vegan is…"

"Let me guess. Complicated?"

At least she laughed a little at that. "Actually, no. It's simple. It's structure and rules and was a focus on my health when that's what I really needed." She came close to me and bent down to pick up the pole. "Sometimes, it was helpful to focus on missing bacon rather than other things."

"Other things like...?" I asked, unable to help myself and certain she wouldn't answer.

"Alcohol, for one. I was pickled in it."

"For one?"

"Isn't that enough? There was a whole laundry list, but that was the star of the show."

Nothing was ever enough when Mia actually told me something about herself, but I let it go. "Well, bacon is delicious. Terrible for you, especially in the quantities and at the level of quality most people eat, but delicious."

"Don't remind me." In one swift motion, she cast the line, and I was transported to that afternoon on the bridge she'd brought up, when she'd broken down her smooth cast into each component part so I could copy it—or at least try to. My idolatry had reached its most fevered pitch that summer before she'd left for college and had persisted until I knew she was never coming home.

I said, "You're why I love the outdoors like I do."

"You were why I knew Lucia would be okay after I was gone."

Well, hell. How could I not melt at that? I watched Mia work the rod, but she didn't turn to me or seem inclined to say anything more. I wished I'd brought another pole so we could stand next to each other and do this quiet thing in parallel, close together but free from the expectation of conversation. Unfortunately, everything on these trips came down to weight and necessity. Mia was so near but so far away, and that had to be okay with me. What other option did I have? I'd missed her for the better part of my adolescence, and now, having her right here, it was like watching bacon sizzle in a skillet and knowing I was never going to be able to taste it.

I said, "You stay here, and I'll start the fire. I'd say you can eat whatever you catch, but..."

"How about you eat what I catch?" She smiled. "Apology fish, if you will."

"All right, then. I accept. If you catch something."

I walked away, but she called after me, "If? *If?!* Just for that, I'll catch *all* the fish."

About half the group ended up going on the soggy hike with Mia while the rest lounged around the campsite, which got a whole lot nicer near lunchtime when the rain stopped, and we were treated to occasional bursts of sunshine through the slowly dissipating clouds. I kept busy making a few batches of pan corn bread and other odds and ends for dinner and assembling more of the wraps I'd sent along with the hiking crew. I mostly hung around the separate cook fire I brought to life, sitting cross-legged on the folded up lean-to tarp, scaling fish and watching the campers do their down-day things: Melody and Steph playing a heated game of Scrabble on the travel set one of them had been lugging around, some card-related but baffling activity among two women of the group of four friends I was having the worst time keeping straight, and the remainders of two of the married couples, David and Sandy, in deep conversation, sitting close together by the creek, sharing a single rock.

My attention kept straying to them, not just wondering what they were talking about so intently and for so long, but also suffering a pang of jealousy. I was working, I reminded myself, and I loved my job. I'd have time for something else, something like that, at the end of the season. I would do something about my terminal singlehood. I'd planned on getting my own place, finally, but maybe I should put that off another year and use the money I'd been saving to not work as much during the offseason. Of course, if I were living with Mom, wasn't that at odds with improving my dating life? Mom was great and all, but she was hardly a selling point when trying to woo potential girlfriends.

Who was I kidding? What I wanted was to sit on that rock with Mia and alternate contemplative periods of quiet with sharing our deepest, darkest secrets. Not that mine were particularly deep or dark. I was pretty sure I wanted my own kitchen, not that I didn't essentially already have that here on the trail. If I were feeling particularly full of beans, I also wanted to make a name for myself with fire and food. And I wanted a family—not necessarily as big or loud as the Guzmans but substantial and lively. I wanted that family to include Mom, but I also wanted her to find her own happiness outside of me and her job. The truth was that I was pretty boring. Under my sheen of outlaw, pyromaniac chef, I was wildly typical, but Mia…

I let myself remember our kiss, which was a terrifically bad idea, but clearly I wasn't as disciplined as Mia, who went vegan for the structure of it (!). Surely, the kiss's pleasure was heightened because of how long it had been since I'd gotten hot and heavy with anyone and the looming shadow of my girlhood crush, but I still shivered at the memory. Even just when she'd held my hand in hers, at the end, willing me to understand something she refused to explain, my skin had thrilled to her touch. Her weight on me had been so luscious, and my gut clenched at the memory, the back of my knife halfway down a fish, my scaling momentarily forgotten.

David and Sandy were so close together that their shoulders were touching, which gave me pause. What was going on there? I tried to remember if those two couples had registered for the tour together and, so, would have known each other before we'd taken off from that first trailhead, but Lucia and Venus were the ones who kept up with those kinds of details. I couldn't help but be a little suspicious, but then, as if in response to my heavy gaze, they shifted apart, each stretching in a different (guilty?) way.

I went back to scaling my fish, thinking about herbs and wishing for lemon and telling myself to move on. I opened the package of banana leaves I'd been carrying and set them out to wrap each whole fish in. Now that the rain was done, I would build up the fire over these buried treasures of savory packages and let them cook and steam in their own juices until dinner.

I could be happy with making this food and having Mia just being friendly with me, having her back in my life for the time being in whatever limited way she would allow. It was so much more than what I'd had before, filling in the deep chasm her leaving had opened up in me that I hadn't even let myself recognize until she was back. I craved to dig into her mystery and feel her tight against me again, and though Mia was apparently an expert at being careful about what she wanted, I was right there behind her.

* * *

The days peeled off like squares from a toilet paper roll, fundamentally the same but satisfying nonetheless. Venus joined us for one night, driving to the closest trailhead and helping me lug a cooler the mile from her car so we could treat our campers to a midtrip party with beer and wine and some fresh finger food I'd prepped the night before leaving. Everyone applauded Venus and the spread, and we all hung out around the campfire longer than usual. Venus historically told the best ghost stories, ones she'd adapted from island tales her grandmother had told to scare the shit out of her when she'd been growing up.

I tried not to watch Mia too much, but it made me warmly happy to see her smiling and egging Venus on, drinking a second can of the sparkling water Venus had added to the cooler for her. It was almost like having Lucia around, the three of us trading off keeping things interesting and moving forward. It was late when people started to fall away from the group, but when Mia went to relieve herself in one of our designated areas, Venus turned to me with a raised eyebrow.

"It's going okay, then?" She'd asked that several times while we'd hauled the cooler over here and had never seemed satisfied with my answer, no matter how many details I tried to provide to get her off my case.

I leaned back on my elbows and looked at the fire's smoke rising into the sky. "I told you that. Like five different times."

"Everyone's having a good experience?"

"I told you that, too. Mia's doing really great."

"I saw that." But somehow she still didn't sound happy.

"So why…" I motioned to her face. "This?"

"I see what's going on."

"That…everyone's having a good time?"

She gave me that patented Venus stare. Even after these years working together, I still was not immune. "That you can't keep your eyes off her."

I laughed. "She was sitting right across the fire, directly in my line of vision."

"You're such a bad liar, T."

"Isn't that a good thing? But I'm not lying. I'm happy with how things are going, relieved that Mia's doing great, and I'm totally in my element."

She studied me for a while but clearly remained unconvinced. "Just be careful, okay?"

"Scout's honor. This season's going to go exactly as planned despite everything."

She left in the morning after I helped her back to the van with the emptied cooler (well, empty except for the accumulated trash and recyclables she would dispose for us). I refilled my pack with supplies and hustled back along the trail, trying to forget her suspicions and enjoy myself the way I'd claimed to be doing.

The weather held and actually improved, leaving us hauling around our flannels and jackets instead of wearing them. Mia and I took to zonking out next to the campfire in our sleeping bags, waking to dew-covered hair and faces and no need to either set up or break down our tents. It was there, with the dying fire next to us, our eyes cast up to stars we could see through breaks in the canopy, that we talked—about the trail, our campers, adjustments we wanted to make for the next tour, food (of course), and, slowly, each other. It was like sharing a tent with Lucia but charged. The two sisters were similar in how they observed people and broke down their thoughts, even to specific words that they used, but Mia was slower and quieter, comfortable with long pauses between anecdotes and topics in a way Lucia wasn't. It got easier and easier to relax next to her and not anticipate either her pulling away or grabbing me and kissing me again—not that I would have complained about the latter.

On the second to last night, to the now-familiar sounds of
Nick and Heidi making sweet, sweet love, I turned to see where
Mia lay a few feet away, her face already swiveled to look at me.
She was smiling. "I'm glad they're so happily married."

"I'm in awe, really. Has it been every night?"

"Just about. I think they missed one. Or I was too tired to
pay attention."

I said, "You know who's never too tired? Nick."

"Hey, maybe it's Heidi."

"Ha," I laughed. "How many lesbian relationships have you
been in?"

Mia was suspiciously quiet. Not just quiet in a Zen, let's
enjoy this pause in the flow of conversation way, but something
longer and deeper, if that were possible. I tried to wait her out,
bracing myself to get no answer to that question or the tersest
one possible: "Four," or "fifteen," or "too many to count."

Of course, I couldn't. "It's okay. Forget I asked, even in jest."

"No, don't. I…" She shifted so she was up on one elbow,
facing me, her eyes licked by the reflection of the dying flames
next to us. "I tried, you know. For a long time. Once I realized
what was going on with me, once I literally couldn't deny it one
more day, I tried to suppress it. You could feel something and
not act on it, right? At least that's what I told myself."

"But, why? There's nothing wrong with—"

"I know. Or at least I know now. But then I was full of self-
loathing. That business degree I was supposed to get for Papi?
It was another noose around my neck, but he wanted it so much.
He wanted so much of me, and I wanted to give it all to him. I
always wanted to please him, no matter what, until it just about
killed me. You have no idea. I was a failure in every respect. A
blight on the family. I was betraying everything I'd learned. I
was going to break Papi's heart. The church, my parents, even
the girls on the cross-country team. My only hope was that as
long as I didn't *do* anything, I wasn't irredeemable, you know?"

No. I had no idea. My coming out had been about as
uneventful as it went, especially given that it was news to no
one by the time I found the words and declared them to Mom

and Lucia and pretty much anyone else who would listen. They were downright bored with my revelations, which meant that I followed suit almost immediately. My lesbianism was mundane fact, but Mia's had torn her apart.

"I hated myself when I succumbed. That's how I thought of it. I let the devil of my base desires overcome my self-restraint." She huffed out a breath I could hear over the fire's muted crackle. "You can imagine how I thought about the person I slept with. I was absolute poison. Venomous." She lay back down and talked to the sky. "But, of course, it was amazing. It felt so right and exciting, which made it even worse. Once I knew how it felt, I craved it, which made me swing wildly between indulging myself and punishing myself—and whoever I'd been with—for that indulgence."

"You spiraled."

She sighed. "I betrayed everyone and got myself in such an impossible state that it all blew up in the most spiteful, vindictive way, which pushed me into the deep end."

"No one told me what happened."

"Good, and don't think I'm not aware of how vague I'm being. You were just a kid. *I* was just a kid. I hated myself as much as everyone else."

I watched her profile. "I wouldn't have hated you."

"Do you hate anyone?"

"People who don't like my cooking."

She laughed. "I can't imagine there are many of those."

"Then I hate the people who made you hate yourself."

"Don't," she said. "I know how close you are with my family, and I would never want to take that away from you."

We lay with that for a while. The campsite was quiet; we had apparently missed Heidi and Nick's grand finale while we'd talked. The insect chorus was loud and incessant, and I let it fill the space between us. I turned on my side and watched her watch the sky. "But you're better now?"

"I'm working on it, but I'm far from a good bet. I'm best with my own company, which is why…" she trailed off, but I knew what she wasn't saying.

I didn't want her to be a protective big sister to me, not in the least. I wanted us to be on equal footing. No, that wasn't necessarily right. I ached to care for her in a way that apparently no one had. "They were wrong," I said.

"I know that."

"Do you really?"

"Yes, Harper. But that only goes so far. That's enough, okay? I don't...I'm not trying to hide, but that's enough for now."

"Yeah, all right."

"You're wonderful, though, do you know that?"

No, not really, but I almost believed it when she said it.

CHAPTER EIGHT

It was the last night of the trip, and I was busy congratulating myself for only bringing the appropriate amount of extra food while juggling my pan, pot, and a dozen different plastic bags of ingredients to cook our final dinner. I was happy—or at least satisfied. Did I ache to pull Mia to me and kiss and touch her into submission? Yes. Did I replay our aborted make-out session until it was already soft with wear? Totally. Did I succumb to fantasy and masturbate to these thoughts with my mouth in the crook of my elbow to muffle any sounds I might inadvertently make like I was a teenager again with Mom in the next room? Affirmative.

Yet I was happy in the most disconcerting way. I was happy to be here with Mia, happy to have her open up to me in her limited way, happy to watch her around the campers and on the trail. I was happy to the level of infatuation, which would've concerned me if I weren't so…happy.

I kept checking my watch as if it would make the time move more quickly and bring Mia back to camp with her group sooner.

It was like I was some wife in the suburbs, getting dinner ready for her husband so it would be warm and on the table after his long day at work. Slippers and a martini. Or sparkling water, in Mia's case, which I knew she loved unreasonably from those few days she'd been at my house. "It's rare," she said, "at least when I'm working, which is never within easy reach of convenience stores." She indulged so little, which made me want to heap wonderful things in front of her and watch her dig in.

Oh, yes. I should definitely be concerned.

I heard footsteps and chatter growing closer in the direction of the trail Mia had taken the group on today, and I tried to hide my eagerness at their return by measuring out water to rehydrate my pre-made green enchilada sauce mix. I already couldn't wait to watch Mia eat the meal, scraping up this finger-licking sauce with the edge of her spork. When I looked up, it wasn't Mia leading the group into the clearing but Melody and Steph, who started talking loudly and gesturing back behind them.

I launched to my feet, so sure something terrible had happened to Mia that I couldn't hear exactly what they were saying at first, but then I pieced it together. "We lost David and Sandy. Mia asked for you to meet her back a bit on the trail where we noticed they were missing to help look."

While I wanted very much to curse those two for not paying attention to the trail information Mia had given everyone when they'd started out—and surely had refreshed them on during their lunch break—I just brushed my hands together and harrumphed. "Okay, no problem. I'm sure it's nothing to worry about." I said this to their left-behind spouses, who didn't seem to give a rat's ass what I thought and were wandering toward their separate tents in a very tense, choppy way. "But since I already started dinner a little bit, I need someone to play sous chef. Volunteers?"

I briefed Melody, Steph, and one of the four friends as quickly as I could while fully lacing and tightening my boots. I was almost to the trailhead before ducking back into my tent and finding my headlamp just in case they weren't as easily and quickly located as I'd made it out to seem. It wasn't the first time some campers had wandered off, dawdling just far enough behind at the exact right part of a trail so that they took the wrong fork and got separated from the group. Over the last two seasons, it had happened twice, and we'd also had to evacuate someone with an ankle sprain she'd been mortified to sustain when trying to use the latrine in the middle of the night without a lantern.

I hustled up the trail, covering ground I'd walked earlier in the day when I'd accompanied the group on the first part of the hike. I'd had to turn around too soon to get everything organized for dinner and our last hike to where Venus would be waiting with The Misfitters' van to drive us back to sad civilization again. The rain we'd gotten days before—and that was threatening again, given the weak, cloud-hampered light that filtered through the trees—had made patches of oyster mushrooms sprout up here and there within sight of the path, and I'd gathered bunches of them to add to the enchiladas on my stroll back to the campsite. They were one ingredient I tended not to freeze-dry or dehydrate because I hadn't yet mastered reconstituting them without ending up with a rubbery texture, which wasn't nearly the mouthfeel I wanted my food to have.

After rounding a bend, I saw Mia up ahead on the trail, her arms crossed, her gaze fixed on the ground where she was probing at a rock poking up in the middle of the trail, digging around it and pushing it with the toe of her boot.

When I got closer, I said, "Bo Peep lost her sheep?"

"Those two are thick as thieves. I think they got lost on purpose."

"I think they have a thing for each other."

She rolled her eyes. "Just what we need, interpersonal drama on the trail."

"We may have had a touch of that even without them."

She glanced at me, seemed about to say something, but just shrugged. "We don't have much time before it'll get harder to look in the dusk. Did you—"

I held up my headlamp in answer to her question. "Just in case. I assumed you had yours with you." In my other hand,

I held a full water bottle. "And this. I thought you might be running low."

Her smile was small and quick. "Always taking care of me."

If only she'd let me. I handed the bottle to her, and she took a few long swallows, her throat moving with them in the most tantalizing way. I told myself to look away but couldn't.

"This is where we noticed they were gone, but no one knew how long it had been since we lost them. I was thinking of going back to the last place we broke for water and retracing from there, hitting up whatever small dead-ends there are between here and there. We'll have to hoof it if we want there to be any light by the time we're done. Did you—"

I fished a small walkie-talkie from a pocket in my hiking pants. "Melody has the other one and will radio if they show up at camp."

"Somehow I feel like you've done this before."

"Indeed. If people are one thing, it's consistently stupid when they get far from home."

"Let's get moving. You start here and work your way out, and I'll run out and work my way back. Holler if you find them." For the barest second, it was like she was going to kiss me goodbye before leaving, but then she turned and trotted away, graceful and fleet even in heavy hiking boots and with her day pack bouncing around on her back.

I could be cooking, I thought, or watching Mia tend to the campfire. I could be having a quiet moment to myself to remember Mia's lips on mine or the tone of her voice as she'd told me part of her story. But no. People had to go and be stupid or careless or selfish and wander off into the woods like this was a damn trip to the mall. I walked up the trail, scanning each side of me and following barely cleared offshoots I might not have noticed otherwise and that mostly dead ended pretty definitively within twenty or thirty feet of the trail. My arms got scratched up during my explorations, the pockets of my pants snagging on bushes and tree limbs. I was going to have to do a hell of a tick check after this. If only Mia would do it for me, examining my skin in detail, square inch by square inch, lavishing me with her attention and maybe serving up a few kisses as she went along.

Oh, T. Get a grip.

Thirty minutes in, I'd made headway but gotten nowhere, and there'd been no word from Melody at the campsite. I should've asked Mia how far back that last rendezvous point was so I'd have an idea how long it would be until we reunited again. I squinted through the canopy, noticing the steadily darkening sky—heavy clouds exacerbated by the impending sunset. Perfect. I picked up my pace but didn't want to go too quickly in case I missed whatever spur they'd taken.

After a while, I got to a more defined fork, though the offshoot was narrow and not marked with a blaze of any kind. Before heading down it, I gathered some sticks and made a big arrow pointing to where I was going in case Mia got here before I doubled back. It was the signal Lucia and I had worked out, but I could only hope Mia would be paying enough attention to notice it.

I donned my headlamp, turned it on, and set off up the fork. I didn't bother with the spurs off this one, at least not the ones overgrown enough to be uninviting. It was a rocky uphill trail, some singletrack that had maybe been maintained at one point but was barely active now, given the grasses growing up in the middle of the trail and the fallen trees I had to scramble over. I'd noted the time when I'd left the main trail and was giving myself fifteen minutes to cover as much ground as I could before either finding them, hitting a dead end, or turning around.

I was moving quickly, and sweat was starting to have its way with my back, soaking my shirt where it was tucked and belted into my pants. I stopped once to take a swig from the water bottle, but I was giving myself a good workout, pushing up the insistent incline, grumbling the whole way. In fact, I was moving so quickly that I almost missed a side trail and glimpse of a clearing and had to double back a few steps to duck under a low branch and through some laurels to a grassy patch half as big as my backyard that was host to David and Sandy, naked and screwing with more vigor than I'd seen them show the entire trip. At the sight of David's white ass, I practically swallowed my tongue and backed away, making a racket in the foliage that I was quite sure they wouldn't notice.

Back on the single track, I tried hard not to laugh…or swear. Of fucking course. I paced up and down the trail, trying to decide exactly what to do while also trying not to overhear their sex sounds, unabashed groans, and repeated calls out to the almighty. They talked, too, which made it harder not to listen (and laugh). Sex talk sounded so stupid when you weren't in the middle of it all, and guys were the worst, not that I knew any of that firsthand. I wasn't the sex police, but I also didn't want to wait around until it got dark and rainy for them to satisfy themselves.

I couldn't decide whether to loudly interrupt or let them finish when Mia came jogging up the trail. "I saw your arrow. Everything okay?" she asked, breathless from her bounding ascent.

In answer, I cocked my thumb in the direction of the lovebirds. "They're fucking."

"You're kidding."

"Not in the least. I got an eyeful of David's ass before making my escape."

We listened. I saw Mia smile but had to look away before I busted out laughing. "I *think* they might be getting to the end?" she said.

"They're…enthusiastic."

"We shouldn't be listening to this."

"How is it we've overheard more sex on this trip than in the whole rest of my life?"

"The fresh air is invigorating." Her tone was droll.

"Should we interrupt?" I asked.

She held up a finger. Yeah, she was right. Either Sandy was faking it, or they were speeding toward the good part. "This is…we need to walk away."

She took my hand and guided me back down the trail a bit, far enough that their noises faded but not far enough that we would lose track of them again. I said, "God, this is going to be like a perp walk getting them back to camp."

"I'm glad I'm not married to either of them."

"Who knows, maybe they have open relationships."

"How many of those actually work?" She was still holding my hand, and it was wildly distracting.

"I wouldn't know. When I'm in, I'm all in."

She looked at me. "Why isn't that surprising?"

It was all I could do to shrug, with her hand in mine and her gaze direct and unblinking. Even with the distance we'd opened up between us and them, their cries of climax were clear. Embarrassingly, I found myself aroused. Mia and I turned away from each other, though her fingers tightened on mine. I said, "We should go get them."

"Give them a minute. The shit's going to obliterate the fan soon enough."

I counted up to sixty and back down, letting my thumb trace over Mia's hand, feeling everything in me swell with the ache of wanting her. What would she do if I tugged her to me?

Before I could find out, she pulled away and shouted, "David. Sandy. We need to get back to camp now."

I swore her words solidified the air, even silencing the insects that were gearing up for the evening.

"Yes, we know you're there. We've given you some privacy, but please pull yourselves together and come out. It's going to get dark, and we don't want anyone to injure themselves on the trail."

"Okay," David shouted, but his voice cracked on the second syllable. "Just give us...we'll be there in a sec."

Quietly, I said, "I feel a little bad for them but at the same time not at all."

"It can be excruciating to deny yourself something you really want. Sometimes keeping in mind what it could cost you and letting that math tell you what you should and shouldn't do is exhausting."

We'd both turned off our headlamps while we were waiting, and her face was too shrouded in shadow to make out her expression. "You're talking about eating a hamburger or a cheese omelet, right?"

Her laugh was mostly breath. "Totally. I lie awake in my tent thinking about your Camp Wellington and have to talk myself out of scrounging around to see if there are any leftovers I can secretly devour. Then I remember I'd have to restart my vegan clock, and I manage to control myself."

"Yeah, that's what I thought. What's your vegan clock at now?"

"Ten years, two months, and six days."

I hummed. "That's…exact. What about your other clock?"

"I've been sober a year longer than that to the day."

I wanted to recapture her hand and squeeze it. My desire felt like everything to me, but it was so little in the face of what Mia had to contend with. "Well, compared to that, David and Sandy should have totally kept it in their pants."

"I try not to judge."

"Of course not. Mia…" I said, but before I could tell her how much I wanted to be there for all of her anniversaries and know exactly how far she'd come, our delinquent couple stumbled down the trail. We relit our headlamps to give them a fighting chance against the rocks and roots and all turned back toward camp without another word, Mia taking the lead, David and Sandy between us, and me lighting the way from behind.

It was a quiet and awkward hike, and, to make matters worse, it started raining about halfway there. This was part of the job; I didn't have to like it, but I had to do it without swearing too much or pitching the tantrum I wanted to. I spent the time planning how to salvage dinner, entirely less self-congratulatory now about bringing minimal reserve food since what I'd half cooked was—while maybe not ruined, not up to The Misfitters' standards. I hoped that Melody and Steph had taken it on themselves to at least get my gear out of the rain, and I wished I'd set out the community lean-to pieces before starting on this adventure instead of having them tucked away in my pack.

I'd radioed them about finding our lost sheep, giving no details except an ETA back at the campsite, but when we arrived, everyone had clearly intuited what had gone down. Mia took a quick look around at folks hanging in their tents, peeking out through rainflies and half-open zippers and said, "I'll take care of everyone if you can figure out dinner. It's getting pretty late."

I had my headlamp pointed at her neck and chest to keep the glare out of her eyes, but her tight-lipped frown was clear in the light's periphery. I didn't remotely envy her. "Of course. Will do."

Melody had done an admirable job stuffing firewood in various tents to keep it dry and had sealed up whatever food bags I'd opened and tucked them next to my gear. While I moved around to get the community lean-to set up and a fire started there, I couldn't tell what was worse, the rain or the palpable tenseness that had settled over the camp. In this day and age of online reviews, something like this could ruin us, and we had to figure out a way to salvage this evening and tomorrow for at least the campers whose marriages weren't crumbling. Though I enjoyed a pretty serious love affair with mushrooms, especially those I'd foraged myself, I doubted they would be sufficient to smooth this over with the group.

Dessert, on the other hand, was a different story, and I sat for a few minutes in my tent with all of my supplies spread out around me and brainstormed to come up with something undeniably fantastic. In the middle of my food MacGyvering, Mia ducked inside, squatting near the entrance. She was completely drenched and tried to stay as far away from my dry gear as she could.

She said, "Well, this is fun."

"If fun is code for something else entirely, then yes."

"I have a solution for tonight, but it means giving up your tent."

She explained what I could only understand as tent musical chairs. Or the great tent migration. A grand reshuffling of people to let the aggrieved spouses have our tents while keeping David and Sandy separated, which felt like closing the barn door after the horses had escaped. I wasn't directly involved in this mess, so who was I to criticize?

"The good news is that everyone wanted to make sure we had tents to be in, so they're not blaming us."

"That's a relief, but now I'm waiting for the bad news."

"They put us in a tent together, which totally makes sense from their perspective, but I thought I'd just move to the lean-to when everyone settles down."

"Isn't it supposed to get windy tonight? You'll be soaked. Stay in the tent."

"I don't think that's—"

"You're staying in the tent, Mia," I said, my voice raised. "Sorry. We're adults. It's not like either of us has had a lock on our tent zippers out here. I'm pretty sure we can control ourselves better than David and Sandy."

She nodded but looked grim, and I didn't feel nearly as confident as I'd made myself sound. "How are things going here?"

"I think we'll be short on dinner and long on dessert to try to smooth things over. You still have some ingredients in your pack, right? Freeze dried raspberries at least? I'd like to dig around if that's okay."

"You stay here, and I'll bring stuff over since it looks like you're finally mostly dry."

The rest of the evening was a soggy slog. I made deconstructed enchiladas (Mexican slop in my mind, but I kept it to myself) that tasted all right but was far from inspiring, and a whole dessert bar, which I hoped felt like a "best of" spread but was really the odds and ends left over from previous meals and a raspberry-chocolate surprise "fudge bowl" that was actually a thick pudding that I ladled out into some cups for adventurous souls. By the time everyone settled down, leaving Mia and me in the lean-to , I was exhausted. I might have sacked out there, but the rain had, indeed, started to blow in from the open sides, and I could see drops of it reflecting the dying fire.

"Shall we?" I said.

"I was just trying to work up the energy. If only I didn't have to pee."

We coordinated our routines so each of us had privacy in the tent to change out of our hiking clothes and take care of personal business before settling in for the night. In the tent, we positioned my head at Mia's feet and her head at mine, a layout we didn't even have to talk about before enacting. I was thankful for the whirlwind of a day and the hypnotic drumming of rain on the tent because I fell asleep before I could feel Mia next to me in a way I was trying not to.

Or at least things were great until I woke up in pitch darkness with a face full of water. I lurched upright, wiping my eyes before checking my watch. Two in the morning and a leaky tent. At least it wasn't some of our gear, which would be embarrassing. I cupped my headlamp in my hand to mute its light and shone it around the side of the tent where my head had previously been. That corner was soaked, but the rest of the tent seemed sound. I grumbled soft curses and leveraged some contortionist moves to climb out of my bag and get everything turned around while trying not to wake Mia, who was flat on her back making the most adorable snores, little puffs of breath out and a quiet grumble back in.

While I was up, I ducked out to empty my bladder, and when I got back and slipped as quietly as I could into my reoriented sleeping bag, Mia was awake.

"You're here. And wet." Her words were soft and sleepy.

"There was a leak right in my face, and I peed while I was already up, and you know, damp."

She snuck a hand out of her bag and brushed some strands of hair from my face. It was so dark I wasn't sure how she could even see what she was doing. Of course, she hadn't been stumbling around in the white circle of light from a headlamp the last few minutes. "You need The Misfitters' patented camp towel."

"You need to go back to sleep. We both do." But now she was gently running her fingers down my cheek. They were warm and dry against my cool skin, and I wanted to push up against them, but I took her wrist gently and pulled her hand away. "Tomorrow's going to be a long day."

"Every day is a long day." She twisted her wrist in my grasp. "Let go."

I did but immediately turned so my back was to her. My heart was hammering, and I closed my eyes tightly. "Go to sleep, Mia. Everything'll be different in the morning."

"Nothing is ever different unless you make it different." This time her voice was soft but perfectly clear. "The one constant every day is me and my past and my sobriety and the need to make it until I go to sleep without screwing anything up. I've been so careful."

"And it's worked for a decade."

"Harper," she said, but I didn't respond or move. "Harper Varnham. Look at me. Please."

I turned back more eagerly than I wanted to admit. Her face was only really visible because she was moving, levering herself up on an elbow and leaning closer to me. I wanted to pull her down to me, wrap my arms around her, and kiss her. I held my breath to push down my desire. When I let it out, I said, "I'm not like you. I don't say no all that often. Everything in moderation. That's me, but then sometimes I don't moderate. I eat the whole pie."

"I don't want you to say no. *I* don't want to say no. Not to this. Not to you. I just…Harper." I loved hearing her say my name, especially in a tone that signaled abandon. "Right here, right now, I can't believe you're bad for me or that I would be bad for you."

I reached out and touched her, running my hand up the side of her neck and back into her hair, which was in a loose braid. "You were always one of the best things to ever happen to me." I left my hand where it was, tangled in softness, careful not to make the first move of tugging her closer.

We lay like that for an excruciatingly long time. "I don't want to hurt you," she said.

"I can take care of myself."

With a soft groan of surrender, she came to me and captured my mouth with hers. I sank into our kiss. Dissolved into it, really, crystalizing and subsuming into the flow of her lips, her tongue, her breath. The darkness of the tent made my senses come alive, and my hands sought out the textures of the warm skin of her neck, the ribbed edge of her T-shirt, her firm shoulders, and her thick hair. I cradled the back of her head while her lips traced the contours of mine, her tongue flitting across my teeth before dipping deeper inside.

She shifted toward me, pressing against my side, one arm across my chest, her hand planted next to me to prop herself up. I urged her closer, and we shifted around ineffectually, neither of us willing to stop kissing long enough to move fully where we wanted to be. Once Mia had given in, she'd gotten softer and slower, her kisses unhurried and deep, as if she might be satisfied with just that, but desire was building up in me like a stoked fire.

Mia pulled back just enough to say, "Where'd you learn to kiss like this?"

"Kimberly Johnson the summer after senior year. Two years older and a fucking magician with her mouth."

She brushed her cheek against mine. "I missed so much of your life."

"We're here now, and I'm not a kid anymore."

"No, you're not."

"I'm not a kid anymore, Mia." I ducked my head and kissed her neck before biting it lightly. She let out a low breath. "I want you. It's a good thing."

She kissed me again until I didn't know which way was up. Totally better than Kimberly Johnson. By the time she shifted away again, she was half on top of me, the zipper of my sleeping bag digging into my hip and way too much polyfill between us given the state of my arousal, which had gone from significant to dire.

"We need to get out of these bags. I feel like I'm at summer camp or something."

"Harper."

Without waiting for her to say or do anything else, I pushed against her and unzipped my sleeping bag and then hers, unwrapping her like a present. My eyes had adjusted enough to the darkness that I could see where her T-shirt had shifted, exposing the skin of her stomach, which I kissed before running my hands under her shirt and pushing it up, exposing her breasts. My gut clenched at the softness of her skin against my fingers and the pinched peaks of her nipples.

Before I could savor it, though, Mia took over, pulling my shirt over my head and pushing me onto my back across my open sleeping bag. "Let me touch you." She peeled off her shirt and slid against me, the feel of her chest against mine practically making me faint. Her thigh fit between my legs, and she moved on top of me, over me, up and down against me, like she was searching for a way under my skin. It was primal and close and unbearably hot. My hips shifted against her leg of their own accord, and my heart made heavy, thick thumps under the breast Mia was cradling in a hand.

"You feel so good," I whispered.

She dipped her head to my chest and took a hard nipple in her mouth. The vibration of her low moan combined with the swirl of her tongue knocked the breath right out of me. I held her head and lifted my hips against her, desperate for more pressure everywhere. She rocked against me, her lips and teeth and tongue busy at my breast. More, I thought. It was all I could think. *More more more.*

I hissed at the graze of her teeth against my nipple, but then she was gone, sitting up as much as she could in the tent, and tugging my pants past my hips and down my legs with me helping in any way I could. Part of me wished for a big bed with soft sheets and space for this to be easy, but I didn't have time to dwell on this momentary awkwardness before Mia was back against me, shifted to the side so her hand could roam delicately from my collarbones across my breasts and belly, raising goose bumps of pleasure—then hesitating just above my pubic hair until I thought I would combust.

I took her wrist and guided her down to where I wanted, *needed* her, which seemed to be all the encouragement required because she pushed deep inside me without any additional prelude. We both groaned way too loud for a crowded campsite even if it were the middle of the night. I clapped a hand over my mouth, and Mia buried her face in my neck while she stroked me, firm and with a measured rhythm that made me want to scream. Breath rushed in and out of my nose, and my hips met each one of her thrusts. Then she was fully on top of me, her hand pressed between us, her thigh behind it, her palm pushing against my clit with every move she made. The pleasure was blinding, cascading through my body from my scalp past my chest and down my legs. It built steadily, each stroke of Mia's fingers adding fuel to the blaze inside me.

Sounds seeped out behind my fingers, and Mia added her hand to mine and ground her mouth harder against me to shut out her own sounds, which I desperately wanted to hear. They were a muffled moaning whimper, and I grabbed her ass with my free hand and urged her on. More and more and more, the sensations overtaking my vision and hearing, consuming me from the inside out until it was too much. I bucked against her and shook, exploding with orgasm and my unvocalized shouts. She moved against me slowly but firmly while I shuddered and clenched until we were both finally still. It took a while for her to take her hand from where it covered mine and me to unstick my own from my mouth. Her face was still in my neck, her lips moving without sound but her breathing hot and fierce, as if she'd just come, too.

I put my fingers in her hair and draped a leg over one of hers, holding her close to me, but it took a little while to realize she was crying. She did it silently and with a stillness that was frightening, but I could feel the hot wetness of her tears against my skin, where my blood was still pulsing just beneath the surface. I held her until she finally stopped and then held her some more.

"Mia," I whispered. "It's okay."

She shook her head.

"Please, Mia. It was perfect."

She sighed shakily.

"Don't you dare think this was a mistake, do you hear me?"

She nodded, albeit with obvious reluctance. She slipped off to my side and dragged me so my back was tucked against her front, her arm heavy and tight around my waist. I pulled the loose end of my sleeping bag over both of us, felt her brush her nose in my hair and kiss the back of my neck, and despite everything, I fell asleep.

CHAPTER NINE

She was gone when I woke up.

I had slept the sleep of the dead after that orgasm and woke disoriented but sure of one thing: Mia was supposed to be next to me, but she wasn't. Morning light filtered through the tent, and I yanked my wrist up to my face to check the time. 7:30, a full hour later than I usually slept on these trips, and I sat up so fast my head swam with dizziness. I was naked and desperate to find Mia, sure she was freaking out in some silently stoic way, and we'd have to start over again to regain the closeness we'd just shared.

I dug through our disheveled sleeping bags in search of my clothes, suffering through flashes of intense memories of the night before, which existed not only in my mind but all through my body. I had just ducked into my T-shirt and was spinning it around to find the arm holes when I heard the tent unzip and Mia laugh.

"Need some help?" Her voice was light and teasing, and my chest eased at the sound. My head finally emerged, and she was smiling at me, holding out my steaming camp mug. "Tea?"

"I thought…when you weren't here, I worried…"

She pressed the warm mug into my hand before zipping us in and pulling at our balled-up sleeping bags to find the rest of my clothes. "That I was freaking out?"

"Um, your words, not mine."

"I did. For hours. I haven't slept much. Did you know you talk in your sleep? Mumble, really. I mean, I couldn't understand anything you said, but you were occasionally really emphatic. You fell asleep so fast and left me alone with my terrible thoughts."

"I might've stayed awake if you hadn't made me come so hard," I whispered and took my underwear and pants from her. But then I grabbed her forearm. "Don't have terrible thoughts, please. Not about that."

She covered my hand with hers, the way we'd both tried to stifle me several hours earlier. "I wanted to run away. I had it planned, knew the number of hours until I could get in the Jeep and go hide in my cabin. But then you were mumbling, and like, burrowing back into me, and then the sun finally started to come up, and I could see you again, really see you. You, Harper. Who you were when you were Lucia's best friend, this intrepid but *hungry* kid who was always around. But then who you've turned out to be, and it was like I couldn't be freaked out. I couldn't even stay awake, not when I really knew it was you right next to me."

I kissed her, wary of morning breath and hot tea. "I'd show you right now how much I love hearing that if I hadn't already overslept and if we didn't have some very tense hiking in store for us today."

She made a low sound of appreciation and kissed me. "I soaked the fruit and put on water for the first batch of oatmeal. I'll start breaking things down if you finish feeding people."

"Done," I said and half got up.

"You might want some pants, first."

"If you insist."

"Oh, I don't. Definitely not. But I'd rather not share you with our campers." She ducked back out of the tent.

I had to take a couple minutes to compose myself. I wasn't completely sure what woman had just swooped in and out of my vision, and I realized I was waiting for the other shoe to drop. I'd seen other people come alive or change in some significant way on the trail or after a few days in the woods, and I worried about what would happen when we arrived back in civilization, more specifically to my house and the town we'd both grown up in, the one that had kicked her out mercilessly years before.

The walk to the last trailhead was quiet and quick, Mia picking up the pace when the estranged spouses kept riding up on her. By the end, we were all bedraggled and sweaty in the still-cool air, and we'd beaten our planned arrival time by forty-five minutes, leaving us with nothing to do but wait at the edges of the parking lot until Venus showed up with the van for the drive back to Charlotte after swinging through Asheville, doing almost the same stops we'd taken out here but in reverse.

At least Mia and I shared one side of a picnic table, her leg pressed against mine under the splintery wood top while she gave me occasional glances and half smiles. We should've been working the crowd a little more—at least that's what Lucia called it—but given the whole adultery situation and the evening rain, I doubted any small talk at this point would do much to turn the tone of the group around. Mia's hand sought out mine under the table, but after a quick squeeze, she dropped it when Melody and Steph settled themselves on the bench across from us.

Melody said, "I wanted to thank you guys for such a great trip, all things considered."

I laughed. "It certainly ended with a bang. Thanks for taking care of things at the camp while we were rustling up the…" I waved my hand around, trying to find an inoffensive word.

"…missing campers," Mia supplied.

"Exactly."

Melody said, "It wasn't anything, really."

I noticed that Steph wasn't cradling her phone in her hands like most everyone else in the group. I said, "You know, there's reception here if you want."

She smiled. "If you can believe it, I'm not eager to use my phone again. Is there such a thing as too much detoxing? Maybe I need to tox myself up a bit to be a normal human being again."

"Being normal is overrated. I didn't even have a smartphone until recently, and I'm a mostly functional person."

Mia said, "I live a lot of the year in a cabin with spotty electricity and a bathroom that was clearly an afterthought, so maybe we're not the best judges. But that said, I applaud anything that keeps our noses out of the Internet and glowing screens."

Steph said, "I already told Melody that I'm planning on going out and buying some gear so I can do this again."

Knowing Lucia would never let this opportunity pass her by (and that Venus would string me up if I did), I said, "The Misfitters usually has an end of season sale on some of our lightly used gear if you can wait that long. You'd both save a bundle and help us out if that sounds at all interesting. Venus can give you the info on the drive back to town."

Speaking of the devil, though she really hated when that phrase was used to describe her, Venus made a wide turn into the parking lot, and everyone flocked to her before she'd even come to a complete stop. She jumped out and opened doors, talking quickly and so loudly that Mia and I could hear her across the lot. "Whoa, hey, one second. We need to organize the gear so we make sure everything fits. T? Where are you?"

I caught my foot on the picnic table bench in my hurry to get to her, and Mia snatched my belt to keep me from falling on my face. Once I was steady, she let her hand drift before pulling it away, which made my chest squeeze and get hot in a wave of desire that bloomed from my gut. God, I was such a goner. I jogged over to Venus, Mia walking along behind me, carrying both our packs like they were nothing, which they weren't, even though they were as light as they got on these trips, having been depleted of food and water.

Venus was taking gear from people before they climbed into the van and stacking it near the back. "What in the world is going on?" she asked when I got close and bent to grab some of the packs.

"Long story. We'll debrief at my house later."

"That bad?"

"No, just…sensitive." That was an understatement, not even considering the possibility of disclosing that Mia and I had hooked up. Not hooked up. Had sex, yes, but it was more. Or at least I wanted it to be more, I realized with a start that made me stumble and have to get renewed grips on the gear I was moving around.

Venus looked at me with narrowed eyes. "What did you do?"

"Me? Nothing. Why would you say that?"

"Because you look flushed and guilty."

"You'll understand when we tell you the whole story."

Mia came to help with her poker face on, or what I hoped was her poker face and not an abrupt change of heart. The drive was as tense and quiet as the hike. When we unloaded the two affected couples at the first stop, the van filled with gusts of sighs and a few nervous laughs. Venus's eyebrows practically met her hairline, and Mia leaned over the center console and whispered something to her before glancing back to me with a wink I almost missed but that made me relax for the rest of the ride.

When it was just the three of us in the van, Mia and I told the full story of David and Sandy's escapade and their humping in the woods, which elicited all sorts of laughing curses. "We never have that drama with our all-women groups," Venus said.

"I think they're just better at hiding their tracks. Believe me, there's all sorts of sex going on, and some previously straight women who come down from the mountain at least a little bent." I tried not to look at Mia when I said that, but she still seemed relaxed, her arm hanging out the open window, her head back against the seat. I hated that I was nervous, but I needed to get us alone so we could finish the conversation we'd started in the tent. Maybe Mia thought it was already over, but it was far from it. And, you know, I wouldn't mind kissing her again, luxuriating in her body where I could actually see her and spread out and hear her sounds of desire and satisfaction. That, too. Maybe that mostly, but I'd always been greedy that way when I wasn't sublimating my lust with food.

The three of us unloaded The Misfitters gear from the van into my backyard to get it cleaned up and repacked in the right configurations for the group that we were taking out in just a few days. Venus went to return the van to the rental place, promising to be back in an hour or two with dinner and a surprise. I was so happy about the idea of pizza or crunchy tacos or something else annoyingly difficult to make on the trail that I didn't care what this surprise might be.

Mia and I watched her pull away and drive down the block. When she turned the corner and went out of sight, I said, "Race you to the shower?"

"When's your mom due home?"

"I don't know, and I don't care. I have my own bathroom off my bedroom."

Mia took the steps two at a time and beat me to the upstairs hall but stopped in front of the photo display that led back to Mom's bedroom. While she didn't have one of me *every* year during my childhood, there were enough that you could chart my progression from butterball baby to awkward second grader to surly and acne-spotted teenager with ease. Mia pointed at one. "This is how I remember you."

In it, I wore an apron sporting the naked torso of a muscled man and was surrounded by trays of cookies I'd made for the school bake sale. My teeth were too big for my face, though I was clearly trying to show them all off with my wide smile. Nascent soft butch and baker; that about summed it up. "Wait here," I said and slipped into my room. I wasn't entirely sure how I'd left it over a week ago and didn't want Mia seeing a complete disaster. I could be neat as a pin on the trail and in the kitchen, but I couldn't quite get my dirty clothes into a hamper in the comfort of home.

I shoved clothes into corners before digging around in the desk I'd used during high school for a picture I knew was there but hadn't looked at in ages. It was way in the back of a drawer behind a sheaf of test recipes I'd never perfected, and I gazed at it for a long beat. Lucia, Mia, and I stood in front of the Guzman house, reddish fallen leaves at our feet, dressed for Halloween. Or Lucia and I were dressed for Halloween. We were peanut butter and chocolate, which only made sense when we were together, but we were always together. Mia stood behind us, uncostumed and only half smiling, back from college to trick or treat with us. It was one of the last times I'd seen her, and now I imagined I could sense her internal discomfort within this posed but still candid picture.

With a small pang of misgiving, I took it out into the hall, where Mia was still studying the visual timeline of my youth. "This is how I remember you." I handed the snapshot over.

She made the same partial grin she wore in the picture. "Oh yeah. God you guys were such a pair. I wanted to will myself back into that kind of innocence and happiness. I was hanging on by a thread."

"But you're better now." She nodded but didn't stop looking at the picture. This was a massive tactical error. I wanted to snatch the snapshot back and rewind us a few minutes, but I just inched closer and tried to insert myself into her peripheral vision. "Hey," I said softly.

She pulled her gaze from the photo to me. "Hey."

"How about a long shower? I'll even let you go first so you can use as much hot water as you want." I'd been planning on proposing we take it together, but I didn't want to push.

Then it was like she came out of her daze and really smiled. Her hand settled at the side of my neck, under my ear, her fingers wrapping around to the back of my head, and she pulled me closer so we were kissing. It was sexy and exciting but also calm and...homey. She leaned back against the wall, and I stood between her legs while we traded kisses and breath. With her arms around me and my chest pressed against hers, she felt solid and real.

I could've stayed there all day, but I finally pulled back. "If Venus gets here and we haven't showered yet, it'll be a whole thing."

"We definitely don't want a whole thing," she said and slid out from between me and the wall.

I opened the door to my room. "Just kind of keep your eyes closed until you get into the bathroom."

She cupped my face in a hand when she passed me. "You're adorable."

"Tell my mom that, won't you?"

"Oh, she knows already. I'll be out soon." She closed the bathroom door behind her.

While the shower ran, instead of thinking about her naked under the streaming hot water just a few feet away, I cleaned up my room, making piles of light and dark clothes for the laundry, adding things from my pack once I'd dumped it out and sorted its contents into food, gear, and clothes. The first season we ran, we only left one day between tours to maximize the number of trips we could fit into the warmer months, but the turnaround time was insane for me and Lucia, so now we ended up doing one trip every two weeks with a reasonable amount of recovery between each. It meant we ended up with one or two fewer trips but emerged in the late fall with most of our sanity.

The idea of three days together with Mia, prepping gear and having lots of sex made me giddy, a feeling that amped up when she emerged from my bathroom wearing my robe. Her hair was wet and softly curled, and her cheeks were flushed. My gaze traveled down the belted terry cloth around her waist to where the hem hung just below her knees, showing strong calves and bare feet, which were their own kind of aphrodisiac, a familiarity missing from the trail, an everyday kind of intimacy.

"Your turn."

I hummed.

"Mind if I add my laundry to your piles?"

"Hmm?" I couldn't get myself to move on from imagining all of her just under that robe, waiting for me to untie the loose knot at her hip.

She moved to me and took my chin in her hand, directing my attention to her face. "Eyes up here."

I laughed. "Right. Yeah. Sure, add your laundry to mine. If you need something clean to wear, root around in my drawers and closet. Or, you know, hang tight in that robe until I'm out." I smiled.

But Mia wasn't in my robe when I emerged wrapped only in a towel—partly because I hadn't brought any clothes in with me and partly because I thought it would be easier to get us to where I wanted if I didn't need to undress. She sat on my hastily made bed, her forearms on her thighs as if deep in thought, but when she looked up at me, she was smiling.

"This room is so you." Her voice was thick with sarcasm.

"Isn't it, though?" Really, it was halfway between the bedroom I'd had my entire childhood and the bland guest room/office it had become for the few years I'd managed to move out before coming back from Asheville for culinary school. Even though I'd lived here longer than I cared to admit, it was still one step away from having corporate or hotel-chain art hanging on the walls. Certainly not the posters I'd had as a kid, which had tilted decidedly girl-power in high school.

With Mia fully clothed, I felt awkward in my towel and made a beeline for the chest of drawers and at least some underwear, but Mia intercepted me halfway there and kissed me. "Come here," she said, though she already had me in her arms.

"I wasn't sure…"

"I was thinking too much." The words came between deep kisses.

"No one ever accuses me of that."

"Don't." She kissed my neck and backed me toward the bed. "God, you're irresistible."

I didn't argue this time, just helped us lie down in a tangle of arms and legs, having lost my towel on the way. I tugged at Mia's shirt, and she shrugged it off, but when my hands landed at the button of her pants, she covered them with hers.

"Just…can we…wait, okay?" Then she pushed me back and covered me with her body again, like in the tent, pressing me into the mattress and releasing a deep, shaky exhale. "You feel so good." She bit the top of my shoulder and moved against me.

I was weak in her embrace, my desire to touch her, explore her body thoroughly with my fingers and mouth, was no match for her leg between mine and her hot breath in my ear. I rose up beneath her, wanting her against me, then more of my breast in her mouth, then all of my belly against her palm. She was consuming me like a buffet, low, appreciative noises coming from her throat between kisses and nips, a first or final meal, though I hoped for the former. Then she was kneeling on the bed between my legs, devouring me with her half-lidded gaze, and I flushed under her attention.

"Harper."

"Whatever you want, the answer is yes," I whispered. My room was awash in light, and the skin of her chest and arms glowed with it, ghosts of last year's tan lines at her neck and biceps. I wanted to run my fingers over her soft skin, feel the tickle of fine hair on her arms, but I was paralyzed in her sight, flush with anticipation.

Slowly, unbearably slowly, she lowered herself between my thighs, her breath strong and hot against me. I thought I would die of anticipation before her lips grazed me, followed by her tongue, softly at first and then more assertive until my head fell back against the pillow and my eyes fluttered shut. I clutched the sheet under me and breathed and felt my hips move, pushing up against her, urging her on. It took a while for me to realize the sounds I was hearing weren't coming from me but from Mia, a low-level chorus of growls and little hungry moans while her mouth moved across and inside me, her fingers joining after a while to just about launch me into orbit.

There was no reason to be quiet now, but I could barely pull in an adequate amount of air with each breath, my legs opening wider and hips rocking more insistently. Mia was relentless, and I felt a climax coiling up inside me, tightening my belly and chest and lower back until she pushed deeply inside me and did something indescribable to my clit that made my orgasm rip through me with a shout that got strangled with my pleasure. Good God, what she did to me. My heart was hammering in my chest when she slowly withdrew and rested her head low on my belly, her breath heavy and fast against my hipbone.

"Come here." I tugged lightly on her damp hair.

"Not yet," she whispered and wrapped her arms around me, her hands buried beneath my back.

"I need to touch you."

"Just wait."

"It can't always be—"

"Harper." She shifted to look up the length of my torso at me. "Give me a minute to enjoy this."

Even though I itched to explore her and bring her the kind of pleasure she'd just overwhelmed me with, I tried to satisfy myself with burying my hand in her hair while letting my heart rate and breathing ratchet back to normal rhythms. After a while, I said, "You're okay, right?"

I felt her smile against my skin. "I didn't know you were such a worrier."

"I didn't know I was, either, but…"

She shifted so her chin rested on a hand she laid just above my pubic bone. "We just need to go slow, okay? I'm fine. I promise. I'm wonderful. You're wonderful. God," she took a deep breath, "you taste amazing, feel amazing. Can't we leave it at that for a little while?"

I wasn't sure I could, but before I answered, I heard banging on my front door and shouting from outside. Venus. And Lucia? I sat up, dislodging Mia from her delectable position. "I think that's your sister."

Her eyes opened wider, and she scrambled off me and the bed, snatching her T-shirt (which was actually mine) up from the floor and yanking it over her head. It was on inside out, but before I could say anything, she hustled from the room and down the stairs, leaving me to find clothes as quickly as I could and pull them on in such a hurry that I was still zipping and buttoning my pants when I made it to the top of the stairs and saw Lucia and Mia in a tight, rocking hug below me. They were talking in whispered Spanish, too low and fast for me to follow, but when I saw Venus off to the side of them, staring at me, I totally got what her glare was saying.

I tried to glare back, but it was hard to look peeved when I was still frankly gelatinous with pleasure. I made a sharp shrug and mouthed, "What?"

She shook her head.

I took the stairs slowly, but Mia and Lucia were still hugging when I got to them, one of Lucia's crutches fallen to the ground, the other leaning precariously against her ribs. Without a word, Venus and I went into the kitchen to give them a minute.

"Don't even tell me," Venus said.

"There's nothing to tell."

She made a scoffing sound, which was better than Mom's. Honestly, I couldn't wait for her to have kids because she was already such a mother—and it would redirect her scolding heat away from me for once. "I can't believe you fucked her."

I hadn't yet, which was frustrating, but Venus most definitely wasn't looking for details. Before I could think fully through the words, I said, "It wasn't fucking."

"You went from thinking she was off or damaged or going to drive everyone away to getting in her pants in, what, a week? Or was it even faster?"

"It's not like that."

"Then what's it like?"

I shoved my hands in my pockets and shook my head.

"What, are you in love with her or something?"

As hard as I tried, I couldn't meet Venus's stare.

"Are you kidding me?"

"I don't know what it is, okay? It's only been, like, a minute, but I worshipped her when I was a kid. I was devoted to her and that whole family. And now—" I cut myself off when I heard Lucia crutching in our direction.

When Lucia crossed the threshold into the kitchen, she said, "Can you guys believe she's actually here? We talk, but I've only seen her, what, twice in the last five years?"

I said, "I can't believe *you're* here. How did Venus convince your mom to let you out of her sight?" At the mention of Mami Guzman, I saw Mia wrap her arms around herself and study her bare feet. I wanted to kick myself for my stupidity.

"Oh, I've done a good job of driving her crazy since I got out of the hospital. We both needed a break. But, man, I gotta sit down. This thing is no joke." She tapped her knuckles against her cast.

We settled her at the table, her leg propped up on the seat next to her. I went to get an extra chair, but Mia waved me off, planting herself in a corner, her back against the wall next to our calendar, which neither Mom nor I had turned over to show the right month. I made coffee and tea for something to do and rummaged around in the freezer for some leftover cookies or brownie bites. Food as distraction.

Lucia said, "I hear there was drama on the trail. I want all the details."

I started telling the story while putting drinks and snacks together, filling in some details of the evolution of David and Sandy's relationship that I recognized more in retrospect. Lucia loved a good debrief of things gone awry in a nondisastrous way. I was relieved when, about halfway through, Mia started to chime in with her own observations, loosening her grasp on herself incrementally, warming up to The Misfitters, even cracking a smile here or there.

After reaching the literal climax of the story and speeding through the winddown, Mia and Lucia started talking about the trail conditions and equipment, and I ate a cheesecake brownie bite and thought about what I'd said to Venus. She'd meant that "in love" comment as a dig or a joke, but I couldn't deny that it was at least a large step in the direction of the truth. Love was huge and serious and not something I tended to fall into or a word I threw around easily. But it sure wasn't just sex. I cared for Mia. Cared about her. And, yes, worried about her. All of which put me in a precarious position.

We chatted, nibbled, and sipped for a while before Venus made an executive decision and ordered food. She tried to get me to go with her to pick it up, but I very much didn't want to endure any time alone in a car next to her, where she would dig into what was going on between Mia and me when I had no answers. At least none more than a low-level confusion that was heavily glazed in lust. As much as I loved hanging with everyone, I also couldn't wait to get Mia alone, and finally in her pants in the way Venus already assumed I'd been. If only. I felt myself get warm with anticipation of the feel of her fully naked next to me, my hands allowed to go anywhere, her eyes closed and lips parted with the pleasure I couldn't wait to give to her.

When Venus left, closing the front door hard behind her, I snapped out of my fantasies and back to my own kitchen, or Mom's kitchen if you wanted to get technical about it. Mia took the chair Venus had vacated, but none of us said anything. Mia and Lucia were looking at each other, but their expressions were more solemn than joyful.

"Tell me," Mia said.

"I don't think—" Lucia said.

"Just tell me. I want to know."

Lucia glanced at me as if for help, but I had no idea what Mia was asking for or how to sidestep her clearly serious request. Lucia sighed. "She won't stick to her diet. She's better than she used to be, way better a lot of the time, but sometimes I catch her making flan and just want to smack her. You know she's going to eat the whole thing. Or maybe give a slice or two away at the most. I try to stay on her as much as I can, but I'm not around enough. No one is. Carlos visits most regularly with his kids—there are two now, did I tell you?—but he's almost as bad as Mami."

Mia nodded, her face blank in a way I'd seen before and really, really didn't like. "And?"

"Papi's fine, pretty much. He's on blood pressure medicine, but that seems to be working. He talks about retiring, but I don't know when he's going to. I try not to pry, but from what I can gather, they're *okay* on savings but not where they really need to be. You know that stupid attitude of, 'We're not going to live that long anyway, so why worry about it?'"

Mia nodded again.

"But at the same time, they want us to act different from them, to have, like, 401k plans and shit, so you can imagine the kind of things I hear when I'm over there. God forbid you try to talk to him about any of this because what do I know? I only run my own business with these guys." She motioned around in a dramatic way to me and the front of the house where Venus had left. "I'm still a little girl even though I've been on my own for years. He's just so hardheaded it drives me insane, but then he does that thing…"

This time Mia's nod was paired with a small smile. "*Tú eres mi razón de ser.*"

"Yes! It's infuriating that it still gets to me."

You are my reason for being is what Papi Guzman would always say to his children, boy and girl, young and old. He said it to me, just once, not long after Mia was ex-communicated, now that I thought about it, and I understood what Lucia was saying. Who wouldn't melt at that and love the man beyond reason?

"Okay," Mia said, but that word bore no relation to the hard frown on her face.

"I don't know why you make me do that," Lucia said.

"I need to know. I need to know everything."

"God, Mia," Lucia said in such a sudden shout that I jumped from where I'd been trying to sit inconspicuously. "Why don't you just lie to them? We all do. Half of what I tell them has no relation to the truth. Why can't you just play along like the rest of us and just, like, do whatever you want where they can't see?"

"You're asking me to lie about who I am, knowing what they think about it. I can't do that. Doing that is what got me messed up in the first place."

Lucia growled. "Why are you so stubborn? You act like being gay is the only thing you are, when I know that's not true."

"You don't know what you're talking about, okay? You have no idea what went down between me and Mami and Papi, and that's good, but it means you're asking me for something impossible."

"But they're so clueless. It would be easy for you to pretend, and then you'd be back with us."

"I can't!" Mia yelled and put her hand over her mouth. "I'll be right back." She slipped out the patio door and over to the firepit, which was almost out of sight, before either Lucia or I could say anything.

Lucia sighed. "We've had this argument before, in case you couldn't tell."

"You can't ask that of her."

"Clearly."

"I mean it. You don't get it. Lying about something like that is a cancer."

"It's only because I miss her. I shouldn't have told her any of that. It always gets us worked up."

"It was your dad, wasn't it? Who told her to get lost?"

"Yeah, but Mami didn't stop him. No one stopped him."

Mia's back was to us, and I wanted to go to her, at least wrap my arm around her waist and pull her close to me, reassure her in some way that I wasn't about to release her to her worst thoughts, and that I accepted everything about her, but how could I do that with Lucia right here? It was one thing for Venus to figure out that Mia and I were sleeping together, but I honestly couldn't imagine what Lucia would think if she knew. It was too early for any of this, but when had stuff in my life happened according to a proper timeline?

With a monumental effort, I wrenched my gaze from Mia back to Lucia. "She did awesome with the campers. A total lifesaver."

"I told you. I can't believe you doubted me."

"She's…"

Lucia waved a hand to cut me off even though I didn't know what I was going to say. "I know. She's been through a lot, and she really doesn't want to talk about it. She just wants to be my sister, and that's okay with me. I wish she'd either figure out a way to cut ties as much as my parents did and be happy or to come back, but she's also made it super clear that it's her life, and she does things her way. But also that she'll do anything for me."

"Has she ever told you everything that happened when things blew up?"

"No, and she's right that I don't want to know. She's got other people for that. I think she doesn't want to put me in a position to have to choose between her and the rest of my family. She just wants to be my big sister and focus on that."

But who else did Mia have? I hated this conversation, not only because it reminded me of what Mia had gone through but also because it made me realize how little I actually knew her. Did she have friends she confided in? People who had gone through the ups and downs of recovery with her? Probably a sponsor, but did she have a found family?

I felt Venus's disapproval eat into my gut and give me heartburn. It was more than sex, but how much more? I wanted to know everything about Mia, but what if she wanted to treat me like she was treating Lucia? Would she always hold me at a distance, even if that distance was less now than it had been before? And if not, how would I feel about knowing what she was so reluctant to tell anyone else?

Probably because she heard Venus's car drive up, Mia slipped back into the kitchen moments before Venus banged through the front door, carrying bags of food. Mia bypassed us to help her. "Tacos!" she called out from the living room.

"And beer!" Venus said.

My stomach grumbled comically at the sound and smell of dinner. All serious conversation was over, but Mia was quiet when she finally consented to sit in a spare chair, squeezed between me and Venus. Her tacos were sad-looking, little piles of black beans sprinkled with onions and cilantro. I kept pushing salsas and hot sauce on her, sliding over slices of avocado and a little pile of shredded lettuce until she put her hand briefly on my thigh and said, "I'm fine. It's about the company, not the food."

But we were all drinking beer and eating meat and generally being our raucous post-tour selves while Mia sipped at sparkling water and ate what I considered to be one step above gruel. It wasn't that hard to make a delicious vegan taco; these folks had just been lazy. What about sweet potato? Portabellos? Tofu or tempeh? You could even do something wild like cauliflower steaks marinated in a mojo sauce or a deep chili rub. Hell, at least throw something pickled on top.

I shifted back from the table. "I'm going to make you something actually good."

"Don't." The word was as sharp as it was short, and it made everyone look at us. She softened. "Really, T. Don't worry about it." I hated that she used my nickname now. "I was about to take off, anyway."

"What do you mean?" Lucia and I asked in tandem.

"I need to go sleep in my bed for a couple of nights before gearing up for the next group. You know, recharge a little." She got up, half a sad taco still on her plate. I sat frozen in my chair when she went over to Lucia and gave her a tight hug, getting the back of the chair in the process. They whispered to each other in Spanish before Mia disengaged, waved in the general direction of Venus and me, and walked out of the kitchen.

"Hey," I said and followed her.

"I'll be back the day after tomorrow to handle the gear. It can wait until then to get cleaned up if you don't mind unpacking some of it."

"You think I'm worried about the gear?" I tried to keep my voice down but hustled us through the door before I went on. "What's happening? I thought…" Then I couldn't say the words. *I thought you were going to stay with me. I thought you* wanted *to stay with me.*

"I just need some time alone. I'm used to a lot of that, you know. It's hard for me to think around other people."

"Maybe you shouldn't be thinking as much as you do."

She smiled, but it was a paltry showing. "I know what I need to do to take care of myself."

"And that doesn't include being around me."

"Come here." She pulled me into a hug. "You're wonderful, trying to feed me, kissing me like you do, but being here is a lot. A lot, a lot. So I need to go. Now." She squeezed me and dipped her head to kiss my neck and take a deep, noisy inhale. Then she was down off the porch and walking to her Jeep, saying, "I'll see you in a couple of days. Call if there's an emergency. And don't worry."

She didn't look back at me before she got in the driver's seat and pulled away. Well, shit.

CHAPTER TEN

Mia returned when she'd said she would but was all business, sleeping on the pull-out couch at Mom's insistence and giving me no indication that she would be amenable to my visiting her there in the night. The second trip was always so much easier than the first—at least for me. My nervousness was gone, and all my little mistakes had already been left on the trail. The route was clear, so much of the prep had been completed before the first trip, and the weather forecast was looking fine. I dealt with food, Mia dealt with gear, and when we got started with the new group, she was professionally friendly to me and the other campers, exactly the way she'd been on the first trip, and I promised myself I wouldn't go to her, no matter how much I wanted to. I didn't know what had happened besides her being spooked by seeing Lucia and hearing about her family, but I wasn't sure how that affected us. I curled up in my sleeping bag and tried to distract myself by walking through the menu for the next day, anything to keep from thinking about Mia in the next tent over, changing out of her hiking gear and slipping into her sleeping bag, her hair in the loose braid she always put it in before bed.

I was just asleep when the zipper to my tent woke me, and I had my arms open to her before I could think. Then I was lost in her smell and the softness of her skin and the way she burrowed against me, always seeming to be looking for more, which was exactly what I wanted to give. She let me undress her more every night until I finally got her fully naked against me at the end of the trip. It was as wonderful as I'd imagined, but she was still shy about being touched. She would bear it for a while, my mouth on her breast or hand on her hip before turning the tables again.

Every time, in a breathless afterward, I'd say, "I want more. You need to let me touch you."

"I know. I will. Just enjoy this, okay? You take care of everyone else all the time. You feed me incredible food and worry about me and want things to be equal and fair. Things aren't fair, Harper, but it's in your favor right now."

But it wasn't, not really, not with how running my hands over her and getting even the most muted response turned me on like nothing else. Still, I was careful with her, happy to take what I could get—at least until after the third trip, when Mom came home from the hospital to find me alone at the kitchen table, drinking the last sips of a Mexican hot chocolate and surfing the web for recipe inspiration.

She sat next to me. "Spill it."

"Do you think I could make lobster thermidor on the trail or is that just totally insane? Lobster would be next level, though. Maybe I could at least figure out a really good lobster mac and cheese. Now that's a crowd-pleaser."

"What would you make for Mia?"

"I've been tinkering with a vegan mac and cheese, but it's still in science-experiment phase. I just don't like the versions I've found out there."

When she hummed, I knew I'd fallen right into her trap by answering that with no hesitation. Not only answering but admitting that I'd been spending a lot of time thinking about the answer, *working* on it.

I said, "It's only the right thing to do."

"Of course, especially considering that you're in love with her."

I shook my head. "That's ridiculous."

"I can see it in your face."

"Come on. You think you can tell everything about me by the tone of my voice or the exact degree of my frown."

"I'm your mother."

"Right, exactly, not some mind reader or clairvoyant." I was verging into brat territory, which was a comfortable place to be with Mom, but I was unnerved by her certainty. I didn't even know how I felt. I surely couldn't be in love with someone who was so keen to run away to her hermit cabin every time she reasonably could.

"I'm going to make you some tea."

"And you a glass of wine? See, if there's a mind reader here, it's me."

"Don't be a pill," she said and turned on the electric kettle she'd gotten me for my birthday a couple years before. "I'm worried about you. And about Mia."

I pushed my laptop out of the way and rested my head on my arms in front of me. "I don't even know what's going on."

"You look at her like you used to when you were a kid except in an adult way, but she's not the same person."

"That's what everyone keeps saying," I mumbled into my own skin, feeling the humidity of my breath against my face.

"You've been avoiding the Guzmans since you and Mia took up together."

"What, do you have spyware in my sleeping bag? Do you know the exact day and time?"

She laughed and put a warm hand on my shoulder. "I told you: I'm your mother. I know things."

I raised up to look at her. "Venus told you, didn't she." It was a statement, not a question.

Mom glanced at the ceiling. "She may have mentioned something about something before your second trip."

"Because she thinks I'm going to screw things up."

"No, because she's worried about how Mia might end up treating you."

"Ha, that doesn't sound remotely like her." I relaxed a notch, but it was short-lived.

"She said, and I quote, 'I can see where T is going with this, and I'm afraid she's going to get her heart creamed.'"

Okay, *that* sounded like Venus, not that I was going to admit it. "Mia's fine. We're fine, whatever we are. She's the first person to say that she was a mess, but she's not anymore. She likes to try to take care of me, doesn't want me to go out of my way for her. Can't we just enjoy each other's company without everyone getting all up in our business?"

"Why won't you go visit Lucia at her parents' house?"

"I'm too busy, and I need all the time I get between trips to recover. You know how I end up there all day, cooking with Mami Guzman. Anyway, we'll have the big bash at the end of the season with them like always, and we'll all have more than our fill of each other."

But she was a damn dog with a bone. When the kettle clicked, signaling plenty of hot water at the ready, she pulled a mug from the cabinet and said, "Then why isn't Mia here with you?"

I got up. "You know what? Forget the tea. I'm going to bed."

I hustled out of the kitchen and up the stairs to my room, closing the door softly behind me, not wanting to make more of a scene than I already had. The truth was that I didn't know why Mia wasn't here with me, and my bed felt empty without her. It scared the shit out of me to think that I might be in love with her like Mom had said. Whatever the word for it was, I felt flayed open like a butterflied pork chop and completely at her mercy. I doubted she even wanted the kind of power over me she had, but sometimes what we wanted and what we got were two totally different things.

* * *

Each tour was eight to twelve new names and personalities to learn, a tweak this way or that to my recipes to account for allergies or preferences, not to mention my inevitable boredom with my own food from one week to the next (seriously, no more enchiladas, ever...or at least until next summer), warming weather then cooling weather, wet or windy, guests with blisters and sunburn and stubborn boredom neither Mia nor I could dislodge (though this seemed to inflict only those guests I inevitably found the most boring myself). Each tour meant a hefty handful of nights with Mia, either talking quietly by the campfire after everyone else retired or having muffled sex in one of our tents.

It was after that love conversation with Mom that I pushed things with Mia. The first night on the trail, we'd both collapsed into sleep separately after a hike made longer by a detour and not helped by us hauling the heaviest packs of the trip, but the second night, I let myself into her tent a half hour after everyone else had settled down, thrilled to see the relative brightness of her teeth in her smile of greeting. "Hey, you," she whispered. "Come here." She flipped her sleeping bag open and cast her arms wide in invitation.

I shucked off my clothes and joined her, resting my head on her shoulder and slipping my hand under her shirt, caressing up her belly and cupping her breast, running my thumb across her nipple until I could feel a change in her breathing. "Take this off." I pulled at the fabric of her top.

She did.

"And these." I tugged at the waistband of her shorts.

If she hesitated, it was short-lived.

I shifted until I was on top of her, my hips between her legs, propped up on my elbows. "Things are going to change, starting now."

"Oh, really?"

"Yes, really. I'm going to have my way with you."

She smiled. When she spoke, her voice was a low grumble. "Like you haven't been this whole time?"

"Not in this way, no. Now be quiet and pay attention." I kissed her, long and deep until I heard her make the sound I'd learned to love. It was a moan that felt like surrender. I tugged at her lower lip with my teeth before moving on to her neck, the divot between her collarbones, the softness of her breasts and her firm nipples. Through it all, her fingers sifted through my hair, pulling me closer to her while she moved languidly under me.

"You feel good," she whispered.

"I'm going to satisfy you with more than food."

"Ah, Harper, you already do."

But I didn't, at least not in the way I ached to. I slid my hand down her belly and hip and part of her thigh before saying, "I'm going to touch you now," not sure I'd be able to stop myself even if she told me not to. Instead, she guided my hand, and my breath caught at the feel of her, warm and wet and open for me. I grunted, and she shushed me.

Then I was inside her, and we moved together. Her mouth was at my ear, and she was whispering something so softly it was hard to hear over the roaring in my head. And it was in Spanish. "*No pares.*"

Don't stop.

So I didn't, not as long as she kept urging me on. I brushed my thumb against her clit lightly, then with more pressure and thrilled at the way her hips lifted into me, moving with me then against me. It went on for a deliriously long time, and I would have pushed through a burning tiredness in my hand and arm and the discomfort of a rock digging into my thigh, but Mia made a frustrated cry and reached between us to take my hand from her.

"Damn it," she whispered, then repeated more loudly. In the exact opposite reaction from what I'd been working toward, what I'd promised her would happen, she started to cry, apologizing in gaspy whispers while she clung to me.

"Shh. Don't. It's okay."

"I wanted to. You were perfect. I'm just…"

"You're fine."

"I'm broken."

"You're not broken," I said, much too loudly for the campsite, the time of night, and the intimate setting.

She tried to turn away from me, but I didn't let her. The darkness was enough to have between us. "You should find someone else, Harper. I'm serious."

"I don't want anyone else."

"You don't know what you're saying."

"You think I've got such a fragile ego that your not coming is an automatic rejection? Or that I blame you or something?"

"That's not the only thing, and you know it."

"Don't worry, I'm secretly plotting to lace your oatmeal with bacon tomorrow so I don't have to bother working around your veganism anymore." I said it with a not very loving tone and rolled away from her.

"You're living in a fantasy, Harper. This tent, these trails. It isn't real life."

I sat up and searched around for my T-shirt. "Do you think this is what I want?"

"I think this is exactly what you want. Or you think you want something else, but you don't know what that would mean."

"Oh, well, inform me since you're so far ahead of me about this."

She turned away from me. "Forget about it. It's late. Just go back to your tent."

I did but forget about sleeping. At first light, eyes gritty and neck kinked, I was about to get up when Mia unzipped my tent and came inside. She looked like I felt, though it had to be partly the barely-there sunlight filtered through the orange of the nylon walls.

"I'm sorry."

"For?"

She sat across from me cross-legged and rolled her eyes. "Everything?"

"You should be."

"It's just that you deserve someone who's unencumbered."

I laughed. "Like I don't come with the most embarrassing roommate ever. No college degree. An uninspiring résumé. An unhealthy obsession with my freeze dryer."

"You know what I mean."

"Stop being a damn big sister. I don't want that from you, and you haven't been that for me since before I was a teenager. I want...I want..." I shrugged in defeat.

She leaned back, away from me. "Something that might not be in me to give."

"Maybe, but isn't that true with any relationship? My next recipe might be a disaster, but does that mean I shouldn't try it anyway?" Before she could say anything, I held up my hand. "I know that's a terrible analogy, but it's early. Will you just come here for a minute?"

She unfolded herself and lay down next to me, her ear to my chest, her fingers dipped below the equator of my waistband. "Okay, you're right. This is better."

"Stop thinking you know everything."

"We'll see, but no more talking. It's too loud in this position."

* * *

In equal parts, I tried not to think about what Mia had said and worked to help her over whatever barrier existed between her and the orgasm I willed her to have. It wasn't important, but it also was in a way I chastised myself for. It didn't matter, but it felt like I was saying that about a lot of things. Who was right? Mom thinking I was in love with Mia, or Mia thinking this was some summer camp fling? I worried that they both were and that the distance between the two was going to tear me apart.

The season ground on, getting hot and humid, though we escaped some of it by hiking and camping in at least a little altitude. I could feel myself getting worn down, having to snug my belt a little tighter to keep my shorts in place and suffering a persistent patch of irritated skin where my socks lay between the top of my boot and my ankle. At the same time, I was impressed with how Mia was handling the hiking load. By the last couple trips, Lucia stank up our tent with tiger balm, but Mia plowed ahead like each day was nothing more than a stroll around the neighborhood. Then again, this was a woman who had done the whole Appalachian Trail—two years in a row, averaging almost twice the distance every day than what we offered to our campers on these adventures. Knowing that now, as well as her trail name, felt different from when she'd first told me. I began to suspect that she'd forged her post-rock-bottom identity over those two trips, and I wondered if there were any room for me in her enforced solitude.

Between every trip, she disappeared for as long as she could before arriving in the nick of time to help me with the gear and final logistics. I never asked where she went (her cabin, I assumed) or why she went (to stay away from her family, I also assumed), and her going seemed as non-negotiable as The Misfitters' firm but still reasonable cancellation policy. As we rocked together in her tent the last night of the last trip, the sleeping bag pulled over ourselves against the cold snap that had dogged us for days, I tried not to think what would happen after Venus drove us both to my house and we had no future trip to look forward to.

Lying together afterward, I tried to think of a way to ask without actually asking since that was way too scary. She played with my hair and said, "I think that was your best batch of jambalaya yet. And the corn bread." She hummed low in her throat.

"All I want are fresh vegetables. And fruit! A huge salad with berries, and they're not even in season anymore."

"I only got to plant half of my garden this year, and all I do when I'm there is rescue it from weeds. Your call about Lucia interrupted me."

"I'd love to see it. What do you grow?"

"A little of everything. But no eggplant. Too much zucchini and tomatoes like every other gardener on the planet."

I raised myself up on an elbow, making a shallow tent of her sleeping bag. "Do you have raised beds?"

"Yes, high ones. And so much chicken wire it looks like a vegetable prison camp. It's a not-insignificant effort to get inside to weed, but the first year I planted, I lost everything to deer and rabbits."

"Now I definitely want to see it. Prison camp?"

"It sounds more interesting and nicer than it is."

"So far, it just sounds like a garden with maybe a lean-to and an outhouse next to it, so I have pretty low expectations at this point."

"Good. Keep them that way. At least about me."

I slumped down next to her, rolling over on my back, my left half slipping out from under the sleeping bag. My skin radiated its heat into the tent, which felt good for about half a second. Nothing actually felt good, which was especially bad after everything feeling incredible just a few minutes earlier. "I should probably get back to my tent."

She scooted to me, throwing one of her legs over mine. "Stay tonight. It's the last night, and I think Erin and Sarah saw us kissing the other morning, so the cat's out of the bag."

"Wow, you really know how to romance a girl."

"Harper." She breathed into my neck for a few seconds. "I'm doing the best I can."

I had no reason to disbelieve her, but I also knew that if you really wanted something, it was almost always possible to find another gear or a different approach or just a pinch more stamina to do something you never imagined you could before. Though she held me tightly to her the whole night, I was beginning to think Mom was right about too many things: I was hopelessly in love, and Mia was going to hurt me badly for it, whether she wanted to or not.

* * *

As had become our routine, Mia and I showered and had sex after getting back to my house. I could feel her mentally calculating the time and the distance she had to drive to wherever she was going. Despite how rational and responsible I was on the trail, I wanted very much to be a brat. It could manifest in two equal but opposite ways: by my copping an attitude when she inevitably left or by trying everything I could to get her to stay. Apparently everyone was right that I hadn't changed very much since I'd been a kid.

I swallowed down my inner child and channeled grown-up Harper. "I wish you wouldn't leave so soon."

"It's better that way."

"For who? You?"

"Not just me."

"You never even stay long enough to visit with Mom, and she told me she misses you." True but maybe a little devious. "And I think you liked visiting with her before." A guess. Like might not be the right word, but they'd definitely shared some kind of heartfelt moment, however painful.

Mia sat up and scooted back so she was propped against the wall. I saw her look at her pack, but at least she didn't move to start pulling things from it. "Your mom's great, really, but I need to do what's right for me these days."

"And being with me doesn't qualify."

I swore her legs twitched in an escape reflex, but she didn't slip out of the bed or even move farther away from me. "Being with you is amazing."

"But not right."

"It's…"

It took every ounce of will to keep myself from saying, "Complicated?" in a snarky way. Instead, I said, "Tell me. I can understand."

She nudged me. "Of course you can. These things can just take me a minute, okay? What I wanted to say is that it's like when I used to run cross-country. I did all right but not because of any great talent or athletic ability."

"You're a monster on the trails."

"Oh, I can hike forever, but I'm not fast like some of the other girls. I was reckless instead. Or fearless? Or reckless in a way I described as being fearless, probably. I would throw myself down hills. It was this barely controlled falling. One wrong foot plant or a rock or root where I didn't expect it, and I might have broken my neck. It was incredibly stupid but thrilling, and I took it off the cross-country course and into the rest of my life in the very worst way. I didn't care if I fell. I wanted to fall. I wanted to fly off into an oblivion that would excuse me from dealing with who I really was and the consequences of accepting all of it.

"It took me a long time to want something more than that, and I didn't come to it easily." She laughed a little. "I don't think any addict does, come to think of it. Otherwise we wouldn't be addicts. But, now I do want to be present in the here and now and to not escape into something dangerously more, which means I need to be careful and not leap when I'm not one-hundred percent sure where I'm going to land. And you're all sorts of extra."

"I don't know what that means." No, but I knew it meant nothing good.

"It means that Lucia told me what happens the day after the last trip of the season."

"Oh." As if I hadn't been thinking about it, the big bash at the Guzmans' house, where Mami Guzman made enough food for the neighborhood, Papi Guzman opened not one but two bottles of rum, and The Misfitters spent the whole day drinking and eating in such equal measure that we rolled along, tipsy for hours, visiting with the Guzman clan while not doing a single, damn thing ourselves. I could already taste Mami Guzman's plantains. God, and her mojo. It was "good job" and "welcome back to civilization" all wrapped up with guava and cheese pastries.

"I shouldn't have let this happen at all, but you always were a little irresistible. You never asked for a lot as a kid, and I couldn't say no to any of it."

That wasn't exactly how I remembered things, but I wasn't in a position to argue. "Please don't regret this."

"I don't. I've tried, but I can't. But Harper, I can't be here when you're over there, and I can't stand possibly keeping you from them. They all love you, and clearly they've never stopped loving you, but they stopped loving me, so what choice do I have?"

She sounded so reasonable. I wanted to argue with her but couldn't. "Mia."

"Don't."

"It's been so long, and they do care about me despite everything. Maybe—"

She was out of bed so quickly I had no time to even try to take that back. "I said don't. This shit isn't reasonable. If it were, it wouldn't happen in the first place, or it wouldn't go on for so long. I tried to contact them, you know. Or you don't know, but I did." She was putting on clothes so quickly and furiously that the fabric snapped like a loose tent in a stiff wind. "Almost ten years ago. After I got sober, when I was making amends. I thought maybe things would be different if they saw me put together instead of torn apart."

"And they weren't." At least I managed not to make it a question. I felt way too exposed in my nakedness and cast around for something I could use to cover myself. I had only my pillow and comforter when I needed something more like armor.

"No, they weren't. Everything had changed for me, but nothing had changed for them. Thinking that it might is just too painful. I'm happy you didn't lose them when you came out, but I honestly don't understand or want to understand how that's possible. They—and Lucia in a way—want me as long as I'm not me, as long as I contort myself into their idea of who I should be. I love them, I do. I even forgive them, knowing where they came from and why they can't have me in their family the way I am. But their hatefulness practically made me lose my mind before I figured out a way to reject it for myself, and their disowning me made me doubt everything. So, please, don't ask me to get involved."

"I could—"

"Don't," she said again, as hard as a slap. "I know you. You've always wanted to be part of a big family. Isn't that how it goes? We all want what we weren't born with. I have to go. Now. I'm not as strong as you think I am or as I'd like to be. If you keep looking at me like that, I'll end up staying and regret everything because I know exactly how horrible tomorrow morning will be for both of us."

She had her pack on one shoulder and a hand on the doorknob, and I couldn't move or speak. I had a whole conversation with her in my mind, one where I told her I loved her, was in love with her, and she would get that soft look in her eyes and her lips would part just enough to show the square bottoms of her front teeth. Then she would shake her head and say that if I loved her, I'd let her go and spare her the heartbreak of dealing with the family who had brutally rejected her.

So I kept my mouth shut, though I kept thinking that this couldn't be the end. How could this possibly be the end? We were just getting started. I'd just realized how deeply I loved her.

"Shit," she said. "I can't leave without kissing you."

Her mouth and tongue were all consuming, incinerating. She kissed me like she was storing up nuts for the winter, holding on until she couldn't take in any more and had to brave the cold and hope she'd make it through. Maybe hope we both did.

Then she was gone, and I lay back and felt my stomach cramp in sorrow.

CHAPTER ELEVEN

To say I wasn't in the partying mood would be the understatement of the century. Despite how late in the year we were, the weather was perfect, which meant I could walk the two miles to the Guzmans' house to delay the inevitable. I hated them. I hated everyone: Mami and Papi for treating Mia like garbage, Mami and Papi for not doing the same to me, Lucia for being in touch with Mia for so long without telling me, Venus and Mom for predicting this would end badly, my culinary school classmates for having jobs in four- or five-star kitchens and sauteeing their way up through the ranks while I played with my campfires. I hated the rash on my leg and the knot in my shoulder Mia hadn't gotten around to working on before she ran out on me. I hated how my stomach rumbled, somehow out of the loop of my mental anguish and ready for those plantains Mami Guzman made every year.

Mami wrapped me in a hug before I was even inside the house. She smelled like mofongo and arroz con pollo, and I usually would have breathed in deep to inhale her essence to satiate me before I even took a bite of her food. I felt a tug of deep affection at her pillowy softness and hated myself for it. I pulled back slowly enough not to rouse suspicion or alarm and followed her through the house into their backyard, which was about the same size as Mom's but an entirely different beast. No fire pit, for one, and a huge jungle gym and swing set. The place was swarming with people of all ages and thick with the shouts and screams of playing kids.

Before I knew what was happening, I was in one of their ancient lawn chairs—metal framed with the plasticy fabric mesh that made patterns on the backs of my legs when I wore shorts—and weighed down with what could easily be mistaken for a whole serving platter of food. Lucia was next to me, but it looked like Venus and her husband hadn't arrived yet. "Hey," I said and took a huge bite of an empanada despite myself. "Good God," I mumbled around flaky pastry and spicy filling.

"I know. I've gained ten pounds in my convalescence. You made it through!"

I nodded, still chewing.

"You look like shit."

I raised an eyebrow.

"In a good way, of course."

"That's better," I said after swallowing.

"You know what I'm saying. Lean and mean and a little worse for wear." She shifted in her own chair to face me more directly, her leg dangerously close to slipping off the low table it was propped on. "But also pissed, maybe? What's up with that?"

"Nothing." I shoved the rest of the empanada in my mouth to keep myself from saying anything stupid. "I'm fine," I said and sprayed little bits of pastry over the front of my shirt. I brushed them off with brusque swipes.

"Did the last trip not go well? Venus said everything seemed okay in your debrief in the van."

"I said I'm fine."

She laughed. "And you're so convincing about it."

"How's the leg?"

She sighed and sat back, now matching my gaze across the busy backyard. "Good. The cast comes off and I start real physical therapy next week. It's going to kick my ass."

"Perfect timing for our season."

"T, what is up with you today? Do you think I wanted this to happen? But we made it through, and we're way in the black, especially since you know who told Venus she wouldn't take any money for the summer."

I sat up, jostling my plate so one of my coveted plantains tumbled off onto the grass to my side. "What the fuck?"

"Hey, keep it down. We'll go over everything when the three of us meet, but we really shouldn't talk about it here."

"Of course not." I knew I should stop, but that was clearly not going to happen. "How could I dare talk about her here when you all have done such a stellar job at scrubbing out her entire existence?"

"Hey." Lucia's tone was low and warning, and she glanced around to see who was near us. "Take it down a notch."

"How much do you know about what she went through? Knowing her, she kept even more from you than from me because you're still her baby sister."

"T, now is not the time." The words were a hiss, and she plastered a smile on her face as Papi Guzman came toward us, motioning for me to stand for a bear hug.

"Up, up, up," he said while making what I always called his "come-hither" fingers at me.

Any other time, I'd be on my feet and in his arms in an instant, the father I'd never had, one of the constants in my life, a man with a temper, yes, but also a huge heart he'd always held open for me. Lucia was staring at me, her head tilted just enough to tell me that she really, really wanted me to get up and pretend I didn't know what I knew. We were supposed to appease everyone at Mia's expense, which infuriated me even though it was old news for everyone else.

What would making a scene accomplish? Maybe it would satisfy me for a minute, but after that, it would be a disaster. The damage was already done. What would be the use of making things worse—or bad again after all these years? Papi Guzman's smile was starting to get stale, faltering at the edges, and I caved. "I don't know. How do I choose between you and Mami's food?" But I was already getting to my feet, balancing my full plate on the lawn chair and turning around into Papi's embrace, which felt as warm and welcoming as it always had.

I'd never tested their affection after coming out to them, which had been somewhat casual by the time it had happened. I'd felt just a nervous flutter of excitement in my belly as I mentioned a girlfriend from culinary school to them (a girlfriend who had flambeed out of my life not long after). I'd never brought anyone around for them to meet or asked them to join me on any excursions or events where they might encounter someone I was dating and witness any physical affection between me and another woman. Would that have changed their apparently easy acceptance? Was their acceptance easy? Did they even accept me or just pretend I wasn't gay at all so they could still find a way to love me like they always had?

After he squeezed the life out of me, Papi and I exchanged the usual pleasantries, and he called Mami over with some guava pastries to pile on my plate and attempt to undo the weight loss my weeks in the woods had caused. Even though it was thick paper, the plate was no longer structurally sound, and I balanced it carefully on my lap while I lightened its load one huge bite at a time, letting myself be absorbed by the food while Mami and Papi talked to Lucia and me...and then Venus and John, when they showed up. All the while, Lucia was shooting me the same barbed looks, but they were nothing compared to the hard time I was giving myself at sitting here, taking their food and affection while Mia was who knew where. Not here. Not with me.

I was such a coward, especially when I felt the familiarity and warmth of their family eating away at my anger like the acid in lime juice transforming raw fish into a refreshing ceviche. I ate until I was sickly satiated and made excuses of exhaustion to leave earlier than I usually did. Venus had joined Lucia in giving me pointed glances at my unusual behavior, but I didn't care.

I walked back to my house, meat mixed with all sorts of fried food heavy in my stomach, making my steps slow and painful, threatening to cramp me up if I moved too quickly. Usually I'd have a couple more hours to digest (okay and eat a little more) before leaving the party, but that surely wasn't the only reason my body was rebelling against the massive meal. Traitor, it was saying. Weakling.

Though it was still daytime, I made a fire at home and dragged one of the patio chairs over to sit by it, raiding Mom's hard liquor that I first took medicinally, then, when I felt less like a stuffed pig and more like the loser I really was, to blot out this day and maybe the whole of the summer that had preceded it. I fell into the rhythm of another log and another pour, going back inside only to refresh my ice.

By the time Mom got home, I was incapacitated, and the fire was on its last legs, my having lost the will to keep it stoked. The alcohol was doing a good job at keeping me warm where the fire was starting to fail, and I could see how falling asleep out here would be the best thing all around. In fact, a pile of gear lurked just a few feet away. It wouldn't take much effort to find a sleeping bag in there. But I didn't move, not even when I heard the patio door slide open and Mom call my name.

Then she was standing above me. "You smell like a distillery."

"My work here is done."

"Do you want to drink a glass of water and sleep it off or talk?"

Then, of course, because it was Mom and I was about five sheets to the wind, I started to cry.

"Okay, all right. Let's go inside."

It didn't take long for us to be sitting next to each other on the couch, me with what could only be described as a tankard of tea and Mom with a very stiff drink. "This mug is ridiculous. I can barely lift it."

"You need to drink the whole thing before going to bed."

"Can't you just give me a banana bag tomorrow?"

"The hospital's not in the habit of giving out IVs on a whim. Drink up and tell me what's going on."

I took one scalding sip and another. "Mia made me choose the rest of the Guzmans over her."

She took her own drink. "There was a whole bunch of stuff in that sentence that doesn't quite make sense."

"She left me." Because that was it, wasn't it? The bottom line? She decided that I wasn't worth whatever trouble it would cause to be with me. She didn't feel about me the way I felt about her. She didn't love me. Everything else was window dressing, like wilted parsley on a platter of meatloaf. Or Tofurkey.

"Oh, sweetheart. Put that thing down and come here."

Her hug was better than Papi Guzman's, and I collapsed into her like I was a little kid again and my first attempt at a souffle fell as soon as it was out of the oven. But at the same time my shoulders sagged at her warmth, I braced myself for what was coming next. I didn't have to wait long.

"It wasn't a good situation to begin with. Lucia probably shouldn't have involved Mia at all. It was too much to ask of her."

"Mia wanted to do it. She volunteered, and now she won't even take money for it."

"That poor girl."

"Hey." I lurched back from Mom, my head swimming and stomach flip-flopping. "She just dumped me. Why are you poor girling her?"

"Because you haven't been through what she has."

While that was absolutely true, I didn't really care. "Everyone's making decisions, and like, declarations around me but not ever talking to me about them. Mia thinks I need the rest of the Guzmans more than I need her. She says she can't be the cause of my not having them in my life, and I get it, but I also don't, you know? And she's built up this whole life in reaction to what they did to her, but it seems to revolve a whole hell of a lot around running away and hiding. Then she goes and tells me that what we have isn't real, that it's this summer-camp thing, and that I don't even want something real with her, when I totally do."

I took a swig from my tankard, burning my tongue and feeling an acute disappointment that it was tea and not alcohol. "And then you're here saying boo-hoo for Mia and that she's this fragile thing who essentially can't deal with real life down here, so we should all be careful to insulate her from anything bad or difficult that might be happening. But all that means is that I get screwed again. Or very much not screwed, not that it's all about sex or even mostly about sex. She calls me delightful and delicious and extra and perfect and then she goes and leaves me."

"Okay, okay. Come here," Mom said and let me lean into her again, her arm around my shoulder.

"I know she's been through a lot. I'm not stupid."

"Of course you're not."

"I want to care for her. I'm not afraid of her past. I'd do anything for her."

Mom kissed my forehead. "Even give up your other family?"

"Like I have them anymore. How can I go over there and love them and be loved by them when I know what they did to Mia? Nothing's the same. So for her to say, 'Here, have my family,' it's like her telling me to go choke on them. It's orange juice after brushing my teeth."

"They never rejected you."

"Yeah, well maybe they would if I ever tried to show up with a girlfriend, if I ever actually forced them to choose."

"Okay, all right. That's enough."

I wanted to run out and get a girlfriend and shove her in their faces, but then I stopped and got cold, the night air finally having its way with my body temperature. Or maybe it was just fear. Because what if I did all that and they rejected me, too? Mom's hand rubbed up and down on my arm like she was trying to start a small fire to keep me warm, but I was frigid all the way through.

* * *

After the season (and the season-ending party), it wasn't unusual for Lucia, Venus, and me to get out of each other's hair for a while, having worked so closely together for so many months. Lucia and I were historically uneager to spend any more time together despite how well we got along. For me, the first week back was always a blur of sleep and food and some futzing around with gear and inventorying any leftover freeze-dried meals from the summer. I'd play music loud, eat prepared salads from the supermarket, and gorge on TV and movies in the evening until I got sick of my own company. Sometimes Mom would hang out with me on the couch and other times, she'd steer clear during the worst of the indulgences.

This year, I itched with loneliness, but I also didn't want to see the other Misfitters. Or Mom. Or the Guzmans. If it were remotely in my wheelhouse, I would take myself out to a bar or a club and find someone who knew nothing about me and wanted to know nothing about me except maybe how I would feel when I was naked next to her. That was much more Lucia's speed, though maybe with enough alcohol…

Instead of stuffing myself with greens and media, I drank too much in between dealing with all our gear in my backyard, making runs back and forth to our storage unit as I got things cleaned up and organized, tossing worn-out items, setting things aside for our year-end sale, and keeping lists of what we needed to shop for in the off-season. I knew I was doing this partly in the hopes of running into some stray piece of Mia's gear, which just made me feel more pathetic.

It was in this state that Lucia found me the Monday after the big Guzman party, hosing off the community lean-to tarp while drinking a beer from the bottle at ten thirty in the morning. I wore a thick fleece and fingerless gloves, and my nose dripped steadily in the chill.

"Hey," Lucia said from the gate into the backyard. "Here you are. I was knocking for ages."

"Hey." Normally, I would have aimed the sprayer at her, threatening to soak her despite the temperature, but I didn't have the energy for it today. After glancing over at her, though, I noticed she was off her crutches. "Wow, not so gimpy anymore, huh?"

"No, but PT is already killing me. I don't think I've ever been this weak. I'm going to have to work out all winter to be ready for next season."

The thought of not being on the trail again with Mia next year made me take another big swallow of beer. I started spraying the tarp again even though it was as clean as it was going to get. Lucia was next to me, her hand gripping my forearm, hard. "Ow. What the fuck?" I tried to tug my arm away from her but didn't succeed. Apparently her atrophying limbs didn't include her arms.

"We need to talk."

"You sound like my mother."

"Yeah, well I'm going to get real with you, so maybe that's a good thing."

I laughed. "You're going to get real with me? Oooh, let me sit down."

She dropped my arm. "What's your malfunction, T? You were a total pill at the family party, and now you're hiding out with a bug up your ass about something."

I glared at her. "I don't want to talk about it."

She let out a rush of air that sounded half like she'd just been punched and half like the start of a wild cackle of laughter. "I don't believe it."

"Why not? You're the talker in the outfit, not me."

"You slept with Mia." It wasn't remotely a question.

I dropped the hose and turned to the house. "Leave me alone, Lucia."

"You actually did it. Venus was telling me without actually telling me, and I totally didn't believe her, but I see it now. You fucking slept with my sister."

I turned back around and got right up in her business. "So what?"

"So...what?! Are you shitting me? How could you do that?"

"Well, I don't know. Tab A goes into Slot B, and boom, you're having sex."

She hit me hard on the shoulder. "With Mia?"

"Hey, she kissed me first."

"And, what, you have no self-control?"

My laugh was more like a gasp. "What is up with everyone? Is there something I don't know? Have I been a total idiot my whole life and everyone's just afraid to tell me? Sorry, T, we've all known you're too dumb for your own good, but you seemed so blissfully ignorant that we didn't want to say anything."

That at least shut Lucia up.

"Mia and I are adults. We had a connection. She told me some things, and I told her some things, and she kissed me, Lucia. I wanted it, but she started it. Twice! And she got all up inside me until it was hard to think about anything but her, and then she left! She kissed me, and then she left me, and I'm just the sad fuck who didn't see any of this coming."

"T," Lucia started, but I didn't want to hear it.

"Now everyone's pointing their finger at me, like I'm in charge of Mia or your family, like I have a single, fucking ounce of control over any of this, and I don't! I know, all right? I know your parents broke her heart, and I know they somehow love me despite who I am, and I know that is the shittiest foundation for a relationship, ever, but I can't help any of that. You *know* how crazy I was about Mia when we were kids, and under all this crap, nothing's really changed. She's still her, and I'm still me, and I fell totally off a cliff over her. All these decisions have been made that are supposedly in both of our best interests, but if this is what's best for me, I don't want it. And if she's happy about this, somehow, I really don't want to know." My voice cracked with the vehemence of my words.

Lucia and I stared at each other for a while. My heart was doing something unseemly behind my ribs, and I pressed the heel of my hand to my chest to try to calm down. A hoppy, bitter smell wafted up from the beer bottle I somehow still held, and it nauseated me. I didn't know whether I wanted to cry or continue on my angry rampage once I caught my breath.

Lucia said, "Okay."

"What the fuck does that mean?"

She shrugged. "I guess it means it's none of my business."

"You got that right."

"It just seems like this has made everyone miserable. Mami was all over my ass about why you left the party so early. She thought she'd done something wrong."

"Well, didn't she? No one stood up for Mia back then, and Mia's got herself tied up in such knots that she doesn't want anyone to stand up for her now."

Lucia's face twisted up. "I was just a kid!"

"Your mom wasn't a kid. Carlos was a teenager. And we're not kids now."

"Don't, T."

"Why not? Because Mia still wouldn't want me? Because I'd lose your family that isn't even mine, anyway? Because I'd make things uncomfortable for you guys? It's fucking impossible, Lucia." I could feel tears threatening again and really didn't want to cry, especially not in front of Lucia, who was probably dealing with her own shit around all of this. I took a sharp breath in through my nose, almost gagging at the smell of beer. I tossed the bottle to the side and said, "I'm not blaming you."

"It feels like you are."

"Is anyone actually blameless in this?" I really needed to shut up. I wrapped my arms around my chest and squeezed. "I can't talk about this anymore. Tell Mami…tell her whatever the hell you want." I walked toward the house even though I didn't know what I was going inside for.

Lucia said, "Venus wants—"

"I don't care. I just need a minute. Or, like, a bunch of minutes." I reached the sliding glass doors and put my hand on the weathered wooden handle. Before I pulled it open, I turned back and saw Lucia in the middle of my backyard, her hands in her pockets, her weight shifted on her good leg, her face deep in a frown. My chest constricted. "I don't care what Mia says or wants, we need to pay her, so have Venus figure out how to make that happen. And I need my distribution soon."

I closed myself in the kitchen and moved away from the door but not out of the room. The house's familiarity grated on me. I'd only escaped these walls for a few years before The Misfitters pulled me back, and now the whole place was redolent with traces of Mia. I wanted to be mad at her for making my decision for me and taking off, but I couldn't quite focus my anger directly at her. She kissed me. She wanted me. Just maybe not enough to upend her carefully curated and circumscribed position to be with me.

Not that my position wasn't circumscribed, whether I had planned it that way or not. I lived with my mother. I had a job that I loved but that made it impossible to do anything else for almost half the year and that was hardly a stable future for me. I wasn't cut out for the kind of restaurant work that would allow me to rise up the ranks. I sniffed my shirt and recoiled. And I smelled. Things were not looking good.

CHAPTER TWELVE

A month later, I still smelled but more of garlic and seared meat than the stink of fear and stagnation, so that was an improvement, however small. I was filling in for a culinary school friend who was deeply pregnant, a happy coincidence that gave me something to do during the winter months and helped me to not only pad my savings a bit (okay, to actually have some savings) but also find a shoebox of a studio apartment close to the restaurant. I was grooving in the second-shift life, shades drawn tight against the morning sun, up to the wee hours to downshift from the heat and hurry of the kitchen. English breakfast tea at noon and Sleepytime when I got home.

Home? Well, kind of. It was basically a kitchen with a bed, and while that was an accurate representation of my life, it didn't reflect all that well on me. Besides, there was no fire pit or the possibility of one. I didn't even have a balcony for a grill. It was too warm at night and too quiet in the early afternoons before work, but it was mine. It was the next step for me, the independence I'd always complained about not having—at least during the off-season when there was the possibility that I'd find someone to date and have to tiptoe around the fact that I lived with Mom.

I was reminded of why restaurant kitchens were such incestuous places; with our hours, where else and *when* else were we going to meet someone? But, hey, I was getting paid, I was getting to cook, I was even getting a little noticed, which helped me move on—at least temporarily—from the disaster of the summer and the decisions I'd made and hadn't made, both. Besides, I was free all day on Mondays, and after the first couple of weeks getting used to my new schedule, which was grueling in an entirely different way from being on the trail for days on end, I made myself leave my apartment and go somewhere where there might be a lesbian or two. Coffee shop or bookstore or even a bar, on the most dead day of the week.

I was cozying into a mug of Ceylon that was big enough to remind me of the tankard Mom had tried to get me to drink the night of the Guzmans' party when I noticed the woman at the next table over. She was cute in a serious, librarian way. Thick, tortoiseshell glasses, a pile of dark hair, and a mug of something she seemed to have forgotten in favor of her book. A real paper book, which I enjoyed but worked well on the trail only if you used the parts you'd already read for kindling.

After watching her a while, my own tea going cold while I catalogued her little habits (drumming fingers on her mug, jiggling foot under the table, cute little nibbles on her lower lip) and played detective with the crumbs on her plate (cranberry orange scone and...remnants of a turkey sandwich), I realized I was fixated on her hair. The rich darkness of it. Its soft curls, the length, which I imagined would leave it just brushing her shoulders if it were down from its messy knot. Mia's hair. I could still feel it between my fingers and smell the woodsmoke and rain-swept dampness of it.

I swore, meaning it for myself but clearly saying it out loud because the woman glanced over at me with a frown, which made me cringe with embarrassment. This was ridiculous. I checked my watch and went to intercept Lucia at her PT appointment.

I'd been doing everything right, moving on, getting my own independent life, and I had not stopped craving Mia. I wanted to crawl into bed with her or bundle into the same sleeping bag at night. I wanted to cook for her, watch the slow smile she made when something was warm and delicious in her mouth. I wanted to lie under her while she rubbed up against me, marking me like some wild animal, her eyes closed with the intimate pleasure of it.

Though I'd mostly been able to refrain from calling or texting her, she hadn't responded to the few tentative messages I'd sent out in my weak moments. I didn't know where she would be, but I also knew I wasn't going to get anywhere without seeing her. I had to either get her out of my system or get her into my system in a very real way, and she was going to help me whether she liked it or not. Assuming I could find her.

Lucia was on a bosu ball, balancing on one leg, her face running with sweat and her quad quivering when I busted in on her PT session. Any other day, I'd have something either joking or encouraging to say about her awkward position and the Herculean effort it seemed to take her to hold it, but I was in no mood and had no time.

"Where's Mia's cabin? Is she there now?"

"Hello, to you, too," she said, her voice strained.

"Fine. Hello. Where's Mia?"

"I don't know."

"I'm serious, Lucia."

"I'm serious, too, T."

I nudged her shoulder just enough to send her off balance and onto her ass.

"What the hell?" She glared at me.

"I need to talk to her."

"You need to calm yourself down."

I crossed my arms while she slowly got up. "I'm perfectly calm."

We stared at each other. Really stared, like we hadn't since we were kids: over the last empanada, over who would cross a rickety bridge spanning a fast-running stream first, over latrine duty. No way was I going to give in. So we stared. And stared. And stared.

She blinked. "I really don't know. At least not exactly."

"Just get me close."

She got her phone. "I'll send you what I have." She scrolled and typed, scrolled some more and typed. "This is a bad idea."

"I don't care."

She stopped looking at her phone and glanced at me. "I don't want either of you to get hurt, and I don't see a way where both of you don't get screwed over in the end."

"Assuming there's an end."

"I'm just saying that losing either of you is unthinkable to me."

"I kind of don't care."

Her mouth dropped open and fingers loosened so much around her phone she had to scramble to keep it from falling on the floor.

"I mean that I need to do what I want and operate on my own decisions and not try to take care of everyone else. I want Mia. Don't you understand that?"

"Yeah, but what am I supposed to tell my parents?"

"Nothing. Just stay out of it."

Her frown was a folding of the skin between her eyebrows that reminded me so much of Mia that I ached to see her. "T. God, just be careful. You're my best friend."

I hugged her quickly before jogging to the door. "I'll send up some smoke signals if I get lost trying to find her."

Nearly six hours later, I wasn't lost, but I was getting somewhat frantic. Sunset was coming on—it always happened so fast in the mountains—and I'd been driving around dirt roads and up through scarily marked private property for a while with no sign of Mia's cabin, though now I realized I didn't know what I was looking for. A lean-to with a garden. That was as much as I knew, which was stupid beyond belief. I had barely any daylight and less than a day before I had to be back at work, and even if I happened to find this hermitage, I had no idea if she were actually there. The weather had turned sharply cold after The Misfitters' last trip of the season, which was excellent timing in terms of maximizing revenue, but did Mia go somewhere warmer or more civilized in the winter?

It was also hunting season, and I was in trigger happy country, bouncing up and down the long driveways of private people who were way out here for a good reason. Lucia had given me a decent idea of where to search, but that still left miles of only somewhat populated country to cover. I felt like a total idiot, but I couldn't turn back yet. If it got too dark to search, I could sleep in my truck and start again at first light. I would have a few hours before I had to burn rubber back to town to get to the kitchen on time, but I wouldn't have another chance to look for a week, and now that I'd decided to see her, I didn't want to wait that long.

Dusk was heavy when I jolted my way up a gravel driveway that had clearly not stood up to the summer rains very well. It was made even darker by overhanging trees and had such an ominous feel that I was tempted to stop and back up the way I'd come in. Given the winding nature of the "road," though, it was safer for me to go to the top and turn around, so I ground my way forward in a low gear and emerged into a clearing. My headlights glanced off a dark log cabin that just had to be a vacation house.

But then, when I was turning around, I saw the garden. Or at least the beds. High and ringed with chicken wire. I stopped the car so fast I nearly gave myself whiplash and struggled with my seat belt before practically falling out of the door onto the gravel turnaround. I walked closer to the garden and saw a chopping block with an ax stuck into it. The entire side of the cabin was covered with stacked firewood, seamless as another wall. I wandered farther afield, to the edge of where my headlights illuminated and saw Mia's Jeep parked behind the cabin.

My heart was thumping when I found my way up to the small front porch and knocked on the door. Nothing. I knocked again. Nothing. I abandoned my post and peeked around the cabin, looking at the Jeep. Yep, it was still there. Why would that be here but not Mia? What, did she helicopter in and out of here?

And, damn, it was getting cold. It had to be dropping into the twenties now, and I was nowhere near dressed for it. I kept wandering around, trying to make the math work out: car + ax should = Mia, but somehow it didn't. There wasn't even woodsmoke from the chimney. I got back into my truck and started it up to thaw my fingers and face from the cold, checking again that my phone had no reception. Nope. None. Zero. Zilch.

While I considered my next move and my hands started tingling with renewed circulation, I saw something odd at the edge of my vision and squinted into the now rich darkness. Something was bobbing. A light. Or was it an animal reflecting my headlights in its eyes? If it were an animal, it was a big one, and I opened my glove box, hoping I had some bear spray handy. I kept glancing back and forth between a mess of spare napkins and straws and a random Sharpie and the bobbing light until I finally saw that Mia was attached to the light, that it was her headlamp, and she was jogging toward the cabin from the woods.

Not toward the cabin, toward the truck. Toward me.

I turned off the headlights to keep from blinding her and got out, the cold seeming even worse after sitting in the blast of my heater for a few minutes.

"Harper." Her breath billowed out of her in a plume that caught the cone of light from her lamp.

"I have your phone number, but it turns out I needed your GPS coordinates."

"What are you—" She cut herself off. "Why are you here?"

I could say a hundred different things, and they all tangled up in my mouth. I finally just shrugged. "I wanted to see you." Needed was more like it, but I felt suddenly shy, though my appearing here was an impossibly bold move that I couldn't remotely make casual now.

"You should…"

"Don't say 'go home.' Please."

"I was going to say come in for tea."

"No, you weren't. Unless you always issue invitations in a bone-chilling voice."

"Harper." My name was a whisper. "Come in. I need to start a fire. I was too distracted before my run and let it go unstoked, so it's only going to be marginally warmer inside than out here." She led me to the cabin and up the porch stairs. The door was unlocked, which made sense up here in the boonies but still caused a wave of nervousness for her safety to rush over me.

I didn't know what I expected inside, maybe some sort of hair-shirt rustic vibe, but it was far from it. She flipped a switch to the side of the door, and the interior of the small space was warmly lit. Despite being chilly (though, no, not nearly as cold as it had gotten outside), the cabin was inviting with multiple rugs covering the worn wooden floor and photographs and drawings adorning the log-and-chinking walls. A woodstove stood in the middle of it all, but there was also a hulking enamel oven in the corner along with the rest of the kitchen alcove, cozy with a small table and metal cabinets painted a hunter green. Open shelves were lined with bell jars of canned vegetables and mouse-proof canisters along with a few plates, mugs, and glasses. Through an open door in the back, I saw a bed with a colorful quilt and quickly averted my gaze.

Mia was squatting in front of the stove, twisting newspaper for kindling and stacking up small sticks of wood that would catch right away. I couldn't count the number of fires we'd both started in our lives, and she moved with brisk efficiency, maybe because the sweat that covered her shirt and wet a half circle at the waistband of her running pants was making her cold.

Now that I was here, I didn't know what to say, but I sank into the sight of her, her hair mostly trapped under a small black cap but escaping around the bottom in curly tendrils similar to the woman at the coffee shop who had precipitated my probably ill-advised quest up here. I was tongue-tied, but my hands twitched at my side, not just continuing their prickling warm-up routine but telegraphing my desire to help Mia out of her clothes, crowd into the shower here, assuming she had one big enough for the both of us, and entice her to succumb to me in every way.

Without turning, she lit a match and said, "I can feel you looking at me."

"I've been starved for you."

That made her glance at me over her shoulder, but her mouth was tight, and her brows crowded her eyes. "So you wanted to come here and make it harder for both of us?"

"I wanted…Can we…I've been driving for hours and really need to pee. Please tell me I don't have to find the outhouse."

She didn't soften, but she did say, "Through the bedroom."

I escaped where she pointed, having to pee, yes, but also clearly needing to regroup and figure out a way to make my case that had seemed so clear and obvious to me when I'd been staring at that woman in the coffee shop. Mia's bathroom was small and dated but functional, a clear afterthought stuck onto the back of the cabin, which meant it was also deadly cold, the toilet seat a searing frozen stripe across my legs. Across from where I jittered, grabbing my pants to keep them as far up as I could, was a drawing of a vibrant bluebird perching on a disembodied branch of a fir tree. It was remarkably detailed and so very blue that I couldn't stop looking at it even after I was done peeing. I'd seen Mia drawing during a few quiet moments on our trips, but I'd never seen the actual drawings themselves.

It was quiet and confident, exactly what compelled me most about Mia, besides her smile and her physical prowess, and her easy encouragement when people around her (including thirteen-year-old me) were unsure. I traced the bird's crown with my finger, knowing I was wasting my time in here being captivated by this drawing instead of coming up with a plan to talk some sense into Mia, but I was scared, and the bird was lovely and safe, and I stood with it for such a long time that Mia surely thought I had something seriously wrong with my bowels.

I turned to wash my hands, and next to the small medicine cabinet (which I didn't open even though I wanted to) was a pencil drawing taped to the wall, curled up at its corners. It was me. Half turned away, holding a fishing pole, hiking pants sagging low on my hips, my hat back on my head, face lifted to the sun. It was just a sketch, but it was me, and I could feel the easy calmness I always had at the bank of a stream or river, hoping for dinner to bite at my hook. It gave me some resolve, that calmness and knowing how Mia had watched me and had sat with this image of me in her mind long enough to commit it to paper. And hang it here.

When I emerged, the fire was going, and Mia had a kettle on the top of the woodstove, a move I appreciated because it was going to take longer to boil over this still-small fire than on the beast in her kitchen. She'd taken off her cap but now slipped past me to the bedroom, saying, "I need to get out of these clothes or I'll never warm up. Just a minute."

I sat on the small couch, which was much more loveseat than sofa and faced the stove. I tucked myself in a corner to take up as little of it as I could and tried not to imagine Mia pulling off her clothes, momentarily naked and damp with sweat between one set and whatever she was changing into. It was deeply quiet here, a silence broken only by the fire, which sounded like a soft flapping of ignited oxygen and moisture, and an occasional chirping of an insect that had gotten trapped inside with us.

Nervousness kept bubbling up in me but had a hard time finding a foothold in this environment, especially as I started to feel the warmth from the woodstove, which could probably make this whole cabin (except maybe the bathroom) toasty even during the coldest night. A rug was spread on the floor right in front of it, and how could I not think about lying there with Mia, running my hands over her firelight-tinged skin, warmth around us and between us.

Mia stood in the doorway of her bedroom and cleared her throat, pulling me out of a fantasy I hoped without hope wasn't showing all over my face. "I have a lot of tea." She glanced around the cabin, avoiding my gaze. "Like, a lot. All of your favorites."

I tried not to let myself feel a lift at that admission. "I'll have whatever you're having."

"Caffeine or no?" She pulled the sleeves of her hoodie over her hands, which made her look small and delicate.

"Either. I have a long drive ahead of me soon."

She made a noise I couldn't decipher and moved toward the kitchen, her steps silent with feet padded by thick, wool socks. "Back to your mom's house?"

"Back to my apartment. Or right to work, depending on when I get into town."

"Work?"

"Upscale chophouse, you'd hate it. Even the sides aren't vegetarian, forget about vegan."

"Bacon everything?"

"It's not a successful night unless someone has a coronary."

She huffed out a laugh. "These days you can be as unhealthy eating plants as meat. So, your own place and a new job."

"I didn't come here to talk about that." The words rode on a bubble of adrenaline that made them less than steady.

"I know."

The kettle pinged with the very start of a boil, and since it was an ancient one that was all metal, I wrapped my scarf around a hand before picking it up and taking it to the kitchen, where Mia had buried herself in a cabinet full of boxes and bags of tea. Yes, all my favorites. I set the kettle on the stove and leaned against a counter across from her. "I miss you."

Her eyes closed, but she didn't turn toward me. "Nothing's changed."

"Because you wouldn't let me change anything."

"Maybe because everything's intractable. Or because change is rarely for the better."

I slipped closer to her. "Mia," I whispered.

"We need tea," she said.

"Mia. Please."

She looked at me. Her eyes were glassy.

"I came here with all sorts of ideas and arguments and rationalizations or whatever. But I just...I love you. That's all I have. I love you, and I want to be with you all the time. I want to make up recipes for you and watch you draw while I cook and just, like, see you smile at me the way you did on the trail. I want what I only barely imagined when I was a kid but that you made real for me this summer. Okay? I love you, and I can't believe that's not enough somehow."

She was gripping the counter, her knuckles white with it.

I covered her hand with mine and kept talking. "If you don't love me, that's one thing. I'll figure out what to do with that and go away, but I'm too old to let people make decisions about my life for me, telling me what's important and what's not and what I should want and what I shouldn't." I pried her fingers up and pulled her hand toward me. "Please." I didn't even know exactly what I was asking with that word, but I just held her hand in both of mine and waited.

"Of course I want you, but I want a lot of things I can't have."

"You can have me. I'm right here."

"There are consequences."

"What, intense happiness? That sounds horrible to me."

She pulled her hand away. "You're being deliberately obtuse."

"Do you love me?"

"It doesn't matter."

"It matters to me. It matters a lot. Do you love me?" My voice was too loud for how close we stood to each other.

"Harper."

"Mia." Now we were staring like I'd just done with Lucia. "I don't want to hear it. I don't want to hear one fucking word about your family or your being an addict or all of the unbelievable rules you've put around yourself. All I want to hear is if you, Mia, love me, Harper."

She clenched her jaw; I could see the bulging of those muscles in my peripheral vision because I sure as shit wasn't going to drop my stare or even blink.

"Do you love me?" I whispered.

And then she started to cry. Way to go, genius. But she also swayed toward me and buried her face in my neck, snaking her arms around me and squeezing until I could barely breathe. "Yes," she said into my skin. "And it scares the hell out of me."

"Okay." I ran my hand up and down her back, finding my way under her sweatshirt to the tacky skin underneath. "It's okay. We can be scared together."

It took a while, but she started to catch her breath, and her grip on me loosened. "I'm such a bad idea for you."

"Ask my mom: I've never met a bad idea I didn't like."

That, at least, got her to laugh a little. But then she pulled back, wiped her eyes, and pinned me with a very serious look. "My family."

"Fuck your family."

"No."

"I'm serious. I want my own life and my own family. Besides, how could I ever feel the same way about them when I know what they did to you? All of them."

"That's exactly what I didn't want."

"It's not up to you. Maybe they'll change, maybe they won't, but I'll be damned if I'm going to let them or anyone else get in the way of this. And I would never want you to change or hide just to smooth things over." I tightened my hands against her back in emphasis.

Her lips flirted with a smile, not quite getting there but losing the hard line they'd pressed into. "I like it when you get all assertive."

"I'll keep that in mind. Because, you know, so far I've just let you get your way."

"Oh, you let me? That's what this has been?"

"Listen, are we going to just, like, banter, or are you going to kiss me?"

"I thought you—"

Then I kissed her. It was the same as all the other times but also different. I was in her space, and she loved me. She'd succumbed, and it was evident in the way she pressed against me, backing me into the counter but also practically melting into my front. I hadn't exaggerated: I was starving for her, and I didn't hold back. My arms wrapped all the way around her and tightened while our tongues met and breath pushed out of us in matching moans. One of her hands was on the back of my neck, cool against the hot skin there, holding me close to her, keeping me where she wanted.

After a while, the pop of sap in the fire and my own weakening legs made me come up for air and loosen my grip on her. "I was eyeing the rug in front of the woodstove."

"I was thinking it would be nice to have you in my bed."

I grinned. "I'm hoping we'll have plenty of opportunities to try both."

"I need a shower."

"Need is such a relative term. It's not like either of us was squeaky clean on the trail. It just means you smell more like you."

"It means I smell awful." She put her forehead against mine. "Will you shower with me?"

"Mia," I said with total seriousness, "I would probably jump off a cliff if you asked, so yes, of course."

The whole bathroom, including the shower, was serviceable but small, and we bumped into each other while the water heated up and we shed our clothes. It didn't help our progress that we kept stopping to kiss each other or feel progressively more skin on skin. But then we were under the warm spray, close together in the tiled stall, and our kisses were slow and deep. I found the soap by feel and passed it over her shoulders and back, down to her ass, where I dropped it in favor of two hands full of her firm flesh.

She pushed me against cold tile, and I hissed but nearly forgot it when her leg slid between mine, and her muscled thigh rocked against me. She kissed my neck and, with her mouth close to my ear, said, "I'm not getting very clean."

"I don't care."

"I just want things to be...perfect."

"They are."

"No, I mean, I want you to have everything you want." She opened up some distance between us and raised her eyebrows in an emphasis I was slow to understand. "I want to give you everything."

"Okay, but I don't need everything. I just need you, however you are."

In my ear, she whispered, "Tell me what you want."

Holy shit, I almost came from those words in that low, intimate voice. "Just let me love you."

"How do you want to love me?"

I pushed myself hard against her thigh and groaned. "With my mouth."

She shuddered. "Not here, not like this. Where's the soap? Let's hurry."

It was all business then, washing and rinsing and half drying off before we scrambled under her blankets and sheets and found each other again in the still-cold bedroom. I was so damn excited with how Mia abandoned herself to me, touching me in a way that telegraphed her desire for where she wanted me but not asserting herself or trying to distract me from the pleasure I was intent on making her feel. Everything was the same but different. Our newly professed love was a palpable thing around us, as tangible and heavy as her quilt. In our now-warm cocoon, I savored her like a gourmet meal, tasting her clean skin, her nipples hardening under my tongue and fingers. She was exquisite, even before I had made my slow way down her body and between her legs. I looked up at her after kissing the soft inside of a thigh. "Is this okay?"

"Yes." Her hips shifted toward me and legs opened wider. "Please, Harper."

Taste and texture were everything to me, and Mia was earthy and sharp, soft and firm, and I groaned into her. I worked my tongue through and around her, waiting to feel how she responded before changing tempo or pressure. God, I could get so lost in her, my tongue flat against her clit and then sliding inside her, her hand in my hair holding me close. The way her hips and legs moved under and around me was driving me mad. But, after a while, though we were both grooving on what I was doing, it was obvious that we'd reached a plateau, and I didn't want Mia to get frustrated with herself. I sucked gently on her clit before climbing up and laying myself on top of her, pressing her into the bed, marking her like she had me that first time we were together.

She whispered, "You feel so good. I want…I just want…"

I could hear the edge of panic in her voice and lifted up enough to take her hand and guide it to me. When her fingers found me and could feel how incredibly wet I was, we both groaned, loudly, free from the crowded confines of our campsites. Her touch was teasingly light but effective, and I closed my eyes in my pleasure. We were breathing hard, and I let myself be even louder in my appreciation, taking a belated minute to do what I was planning and slipping my fingers inside her. She swore in a dreamy way, and we loved each other, both of us distracted and fulfilled and rocketing up into the stratosphere. I was so consumed by what Mia was doing to me that I almost missed it when she bucked harder against my hand and shuddered, crying out into the cold room. I came right after, her orgasm pushing me over the small edge to pleasurable oblivion.

I collapsed down onto her, feeling her rapid heartbeat in her neck with my lips, tracking its slowing rhythm in relation to my own. It took a while for me to remember time and place outside this woman, but I smiled when I did.

She kissed my hair. "I feel like I should say something monumental, but all I can think is that if I still smoked, I'd have a cigarette now."

"You don't need to say anything, but I feel like I need to thank you for about a million things. If I weren't a pile of jelly, I would make you something to eat."

"I could just eat you."

I burrowed even closer. "I thought you lived on air and sunshine." Her laugh was a rumble in my ear. "Or I guess canned produce from your garden." She hummed. I couldn't hear the fire from where we were, but her heartbeat was the next best thing. "Do you hide up here all winter?"

"I'm not hiding."

"Fine. Hibernate?"

"I like the cold and quiet, but I often have to work. If I did actually live on air and sunshine, maybe I really could hibernate."

"I saw that drawing of me in your bathroom. Do you have others?"

I swore I could hear her smile in the pause before she answered. "Of course. A lot, actually."

"Can I see them?"

"Absolutely not."

It was my turn to smile. "How do you—"

But Mia cut me off. "No more questions. Can't we just lie here for a while?"

I hummed. "One more?"

"Only if you make us some tea when I'm ready to let you out of my clutches for a few minutes."

"Deal. Will you come back to town with me tomorrow?"

"Ah, Harper." I tensed for rejection, but she said, "I don't know how I'm going to ever tear myself away from you again."

CHAPTER THIRTEEN

Sautéing, sous viding, and searing meat all evening while a vegan waited for me in bed at the end of the night was a perplexing but pleasant experience. She wasn't there all the time but more than enough for me to get used to her next to me. Sometimes I'd wake up midmorning to a note instead of a warm body, and she'd disappear for a night or two, but I quickly stopped worrying if she were going to come back. I burrowed into my bliss like I'd accused Mia of hiding out in her cabin, but as confident and brash as I'd been in her kitchen, I was wary of testing what we had outside the confines of my small apartment.

Instead of hibernating, Mia shopped for us and made easy but delicious salads and veggie wraps, and when I woke up, she was, more often than not, sitting in the one chair I had, working at something in her sketchbook. I'd lie in bed and watch her, and she'd refuse to look up from her paper but smiled at my attention. And we'd talk.

The cabin: a decrepit shack before she bought it for a song eight years before from someone in rehab with her who she suspected used the money for drugs. A huge part of her recovery was working on it, and all of her extra money had gone into things she couldn't do herself, like a new roof, some electrical, and updating the septic and well pump. She'd done seemingly a million different jobs over the last decade to keep herself busy and outside as much as possible, but she'd also started doing some illustrating freelance work and was torn between really pursuing that and feeding her need for nature in a very active sense. Right now, she was coasting on the "windfall" that she'd gotten from The Misfitters and would figure out her next move at some point but not now.

She was layers and layers deep, and each one I uncovered with my questions revealed another one I wanted to dig into. Sometimes she quieted my interrogation with kisses, sometimes she turned quiet and introspective, and sometimes she dug in and told me detailed stories of her winters as a ski instructor, which was challenging when you were sober; a summer canning salmon in Alaska; or the intricacies of snowplowing at night, her memories animating her face and making her hands expressively alive.

Other times, she'd turn my questions back around to me, not just about what I'd done while she'd been out of my life but picking apart my desires. Did I really want my own kitchen? Did I want to run a restaurant? What did I love most about food and cooking? Would I be happy off the trail for so long? All good questions, and I didn't have good answers until I went back to The Misfitters and the roadmap Lucia, Venus, and I had put together before the craziness of this season. It had excited us all: the idea of having multiple simultaneous tours, of my training a small cadre of camp chefs and Lucia some guides, of my spending more time developing recipes but also still being able to take what I'd learned on the trail with me. I wanted my own kitchen, yes, but not a brick-and-mortar one.

We didn't talk about Mia's family or, even, much about The Misfitters, though she wanted to hear more about how we'd gotten started and how we were planning to build demand for our expansion. Venus wanted to talk about that as well, but I put her and Lucia off as much as I could. I loved them and the company, but Mia was taking things one day at a time, and I was right there with her. I kept Mom at bay by sharing a few lunches with her at the hospital, but early one afternoon, a knocking on my door interrupted the very start of a steamy siesta Mia and I were fitting in before I had to get to work.

We mostly stopped what we were doing, but Mia's hand slid farther down my back to my hip when she whispered, "Maybe they'll go away?"

"Jehovah's Witnesses?"

"Mormons?"

"Either way, they really don't want to see what we're doing."

We laughed and shushed each other when the knock came again, this time with Lucia's voice. "Open up, T. I know you're in there."

"Luce." I climbed off Mia, who was already reaching for her shirt. "You sound like the fuzz."

"Yeah, well, you're going to be in trouble for sure if you don't let me in." So I did, and she stood in the open doorway and looked back and forth between me and Mia. "Hey," she said to her sister but made no move toward her the way I'd seen her do after our summer trips.

"Lucia." Mia smiled.

"God, I'm gonna vomit." Her eye roll was the height of drama. You could always count on us to slip back a few notches on the maturity scale when we were together, but now I wanted to do better.

I was about to lay into her for that reaction, but Mia just laughed. "I told Harper she had to talk to you about us sooner or later."

"Clearly I was going for later." I closed the door behind us.

Lucia glanced around, obviously trying to avoid looking at the tousled bed, but there wasn't much else to catch the eye. "This apartment is terrible, T."

Hearing my name and my nickname in such close succession gave me whiplash, but since I answered to both, I said, "Hence not having anyone over. Until now."

We all stood around, the air thick and awkward, though Mia was still smiling inexplicably. I hoped it was because she was getting off a little on mentally undressing me in front of her sister, who *so* didn't want to think about Mia and me together in that way.

"Please tell me you have something to drink," Lucia said.

"Tea, and a trove of sparkling water." For Mia, of course.

Lucia ducked her head. "Right. Sorry."

Mia said, "I told Harper she could drink. I don't mind."

Awkward silence again.

Lucia said, "So you guys are…"

Mia moved to me and took my hand. "Yes."

"I feel like I should ask one of you your intentions, but I don't know which."

"I love her, Lucia," I said.

She made a twisted face but nodded. "It changes things, though, right? Some between us, but with everyone else…"

Mia squeezed my hand, hard. "That depends on them."

Lucia's fingers were tangled in the fringe of her scarf, and she wouldn't look at us. "Are you going to…God, I don't know. What am I saying? Of course you're not. You're just going to disappear on us. Both of you this time. You left me before, and now you're going to take my best friend with you."

It wasn't a question, and Mia was cutting off the circulation in my fingers. I said, "I can't live for their approval."

"I should go," Mia said.

"No. This is the most ridiculous thing, ever. Lucia, I love Mia. Mia loves me. We're doing nothing wrong, and that's the end of it. You don't have a problem with us as a couple besides, you know, the fact that I'm boning your sister—"

"T," Lucia said at the same time Mia said, "Harper." Okay, so I was still susceptible to the siren song of immaturity.

"Just trying to lighten the mood." I went on. "My mom's worried but happy," which clearly was news to Mia, the way her gaze snapped on me. "Venus thinks the world is coming to an end, but that's nothing new. We'll figure out The Misfitters soon because we always do, and that's all I have right now.

Everything else is…everything fucking else." I would have dusted off my hands to show how finished I was with this part of the conversation if the bones of Mia's fingers weren't pressing all the way to the bones of mine.

Lucia's voice was loud when she said, "Everything else is *me*, T." She pressed her hand against her chest, where it was mostly swallowed up by her scarf. "I've been lying to them for years about Mia and now you want me to lie to them about you? How am I supposed to explain you're not coming over anymore, you're not cooking empanadas with Mami or bringing a bunch of fish over for Papi to bake? Mia's been gone for years, but you—" She cut herself off. "I'm glad you're happy and all, but you're putting me in an impossible position."

"I don't want you to lie for me. Just don't tell them anything."

Lucia let out a scoffing breath. "Please. Mia, you know."

Mia's face twisted up in a grimace, and her fingers were never going to release mine. "I never meant to make things harder for you by agreeing to come back into your life. I never wanted to leave you in the first place, and I didn't think—"

"Exactly!" Lucia shouted. "You didn't think and now T's not thinking, and I'm left trying to keep the family happy while not losing two of the most important people in my life."

I said, "I'm not going anywhere."

"Whether you know it or admit it or not, you're going to make me choose. Maybe not right now, but it's going to happen. You don't know how these things work, how our family works."

"For fuck's sake! I can't believe any of us have to choose. But Lucia, don't forget that you stood in my house after our first tour and begged Mia to be completely disingenuous to smooth things over with your parents, so think about what you're asking when you ask anything of us." Now my free hand wasn't free anymore but wholly occupied by squeezing the life out of the Formica countertop I was leaning against.

"Harper," Mia said and finally loosened the vise grip she had on my other hand. "Let's not be like this, okay? Can we focus on love and truth as much as we can? Please." She gazed at me, eyes unblinking and a crease between her eyebrows.

My shoulders ratcheted down from where they'd been up around my ears. "Sorry." I took a deep breath. "I'm sorry," I said to Lucia. "You're my sister from another mister. I would do a lot to remain an honorary Guzman, but I won't do just anything."

Lucia said, "I know. I don't like it—it makes me feel like shit, actually, but I get it. If Papi knew, he would flip his shit so hard they'd hear it all the way on the trail. I would definitely get caught up in the blast radius."

"What about Mami?"

Lucia and I looked at Mia. Lucia said, "What about her?"

"Do you think she's as intractable as he is?"

"No, but they're so traditional still. What he says goes."

"Like it did when they disowned me?" Mia crossed her arms over her chest but was otherwise admirably calm, given the subject matter.

Lucia said, "I don't know what happened then. It was closed door all the way. Why, did Mami put up a fight?"

"No." This was said to her bare feet. "But I always had the feeling that she wasn't on board. It was something about how she looked at me—the fact that she looked at me at all. She would never outright contradict him, which I let consume me with hate for a long time, but I always thought that if I tried again, I would try with her."

"Hey," Lucia said to get Mia to look at her. "Even if you get through to her and she accepts you—and T—it won't change anything. Papi won't come around. I love him, but he's stuck in the dark ages sometimes."

"I hear you, and believe me, I get it. I'm not likely to ever forget some of the things he said to me. I just thought...I've always wondered...maybe I could try again in a different way." She ran a hand through her hair and sighed shakily. "Can we just visit now? I've missed you." She took a step away from us. "I just need a minute."

Lucia and I watched her walk to the bathroom, turn on the light inside, and shut the door softly behind her.

I made a motion for Lucia's coat. "Do you want some tea? I have just enough time for a cup before I have to go to work."

"I don't want to be the bad guy here," she said but unbuttoned her coat and handed it over. "I don't want to upset her, but you need to figure this out and soon."

"I know, but it's got to be on Mia's terms after everything she's been through. Can you just…keep quiet for now? Give us some time. Please."

* * *

Lucia's presence had worn a soft, thin spot in the lovely wall I'd put around Mia and me. That spot tempted idle fingers, and Mia—and I—couldn't stop worrying at it. Lucia had sat with us, drunk tea, and had unwound and relaxed at least a notch before she'd left for PT, I'd gone to work, and Mia had escaped to her cabin to be by herself—but, surprisingly, only for one night. She was in my bed but not asleep when I got home from work the next day and held the covers open for me to climb into after I'd taken a shower. We shuffled around so I had her back to my front, my arm around her chest, hand between her breasts.

"Even though it's what I did for years, you know we can't hide from it," she said.

"I totally see the allure of your cabin now."

"I know, right?"

I was exhausted from work and wanted nothing more than to sink into her warmth and sleep away everything outside the two of us, but Mia wasn't having it. "You can still have a relationship with them. I can handle it. I'll step aside for that however much you want me to."

"No."

"Harper, don't be stubborn."

"Stubborn? That's some real pot and kettle shit going on. What's it going to take to get through your head that we're in this together? You're not stepping aside. You're not suffering in silence. Not on my watch. No way, no how."

In the sudden quiet after that outburst, the swish of traffic outside on the main drag filtered through my window. Even in the dead of night, someone was always going somewhere. I felt her shoulders shake a little and cursed myself that I'd made her cry again, but I finally realized she was laughing—trying not to but definitely laughing.

"No way, no how?" she said and just howled with it.

"Okay, all right. Clearly I lived with my mother too long."

She turned around and put her hand on me, half on my neck and half on my jaw. "I know I just offered to step aside, but I want to try again. If I can just focus on Mami, if I can have you with me, if she can see how happy we are, maybe she'll remember that she loved me."

"And if it goes like Lucia thinks it will? I don't know if I can stand by while you get hurt again. It kills me to see you when you're upset."

She kissed me. "Too bad I'm my own woman who makes her own decisions. I'm still working this out, but I won't do anything if you can't be there with me. Just please be with me. Can you do that?"

"Of course. I'm kind of offended you even asked."

"This is a lot. I've tried to do it by myself before, and I can't do it that way again. There's so much history on my side, but now, being with you, I need to see. I need to be sure. If there's a way, I want to try even as I don't want to go through it again, okay? I don't want to see them and watch their faces curdle with disappointment. But if I don't, I'll always wonder, now that I know how much they just adore you despite everything. Not that I blame them."

"This is going to go so terribly."

"I know, and I'm ready for it." I must've shown my uncertainty because she reached out to me again, tucking hair behind my ear and running a thumb across my lips. "I can handle it, Harper. Maybe not before, but with you here I feel like I can handle anything. I don't want you with me just for this. I want you with me no matter what happens."

"You've got me. You always did."

* * *

The next week was filled with calls between Mia and Lucia, some kind of sisterly scheming or advice or maybe just swapping gossip for all I knew. They only sometimes talked when I wasn't at the restaurant, and when they did, Mia was quiet but not secretive. She had clearly decided to do this, and I tried to ready myself to stand still in front of a speeding freight train. Ironically, I loved to see this kind of determination in Mia. She was lit up with purpose in a way I'd sometimes seen on the trail when she was working the hatchet or listening intently to the weather radio. It rekindled my spark of devotion to The Misfitters and my excitement about our plans. Because of our reviews and Venus and Lucia's efforts on social media, there was the growing possibility that we'd have more demand than we could meet with our current tour schedule. Just how much more was yet to be seen, but I started to work on making sure all my camp recipes were written down as much as they could be, given the vicissitudes of fire.

Then, on one of my Mondays off, Mia and I stood outside of the house I'd spent so much time at while I was growing up, the house I'd practically run from a couple months earlier. I'd called, and Mami was expecting me. Me, not us. I had no idea if Papi would be there, but Mia was in a dress and tights, and I wore actual pants and a sweater, and this time I was squeezing the life out of *her* hand. Our breath plumed out in front of us, pale in the winter sunlight, and I rang the doorbell and waited.

"I love you," Mia whispered, and I could barely breathe.

Mami opened the door, smiled at me, and…stopped smiling when she saw Mia. Her expression wasn't angry (believe me, Lucia and I had been in trouble enough that I had plenty of experience with that one), but it was far from her usual jolly self. Time slowed, and I could smell onions and garlic and cilantro wafting out from the house behind her along with heat Papi would be yelling about paying for. But Papi wasn't yelling, which meant he wasn't home, exactly as Mia had planned. One thing at a time, and right now that thing was Mami.

"*Hola*, Mami," Mia said.

Mami looked between us, then down at our hands, and her face just...crumpled. Of course, Mia had known ahead of time what she was doing, but I only caught on now. She was making Mami choose, really choose, for herself without anyone breathing down her neck. Have both of us or neither. Have us for who we were or not have us at all. It was a choice I'd never really forced with the Guzmans, not out of any premeditation but because it just hadn't come up. Or maybe, I realized, I'd made sure it hadn't come up. But now it was here, and as much as I wanted to throw up from this slow-motion catastrophe, I felt a growing strength and purpose in Mia that made me fall even more in love with her.

"Can we come in?" I asked.

Mami was shaking her head, her hand gripping the door, and I felt my throat thicken, trapping any arguments I might make, but before she closed the door, Lucia appeared behind her and put her hand on Mami's arm.

"Yes, Mami," she said. "It's time." They looked at each other for a long moment before Mami dropped her hand from the door and bowed her head. She stepped back, Mia and I stepped forward, and we were truly begun.

Bella Books, Inc.
Women. Books. Even Better Together.
P.O. Box 10543
Tallahassee, FL 32302
Phone: (800) 729-4992
www.BellaBooks.com

More Titles from Bella Books

Mabel and Everything After – Hannah Safren
978-1-64247-390-2 | 274 pgs | paperback: $17.95 | eBook: $9.99
A law student and a wannabe brewery owner find that the path to a
fairy tale happily-ever-after is often the long and scenic route.

To Be With You – TJ O'Shea
978-1-64247-419-0 | 348 pgs | paperback: $19.95 | eBook: $9.99
Sometimes the choice is between loving safely or loving bravely.

I Dare You to Love Me – Lori G. Matthews
978-1-64247-389-6 | 292 pgs | paperback: $18.95 | eBook: $9.99
An enemy-to-lovers romance about daring to follow your heart, even
when it's the hardest thing to do.

The Lady Adventurers Club - Karen Frost
978-1-64247-414-5 | 300 pgs | paperback: $18.95 | eBook: $9.99
Four women. One undiscovered Egyptian tomb. One (maybe) angry
Egyptian goddess. What could possibly go wrong?

Golden Hour - Kat Jackson
978-1-64247-397-1 | 250 pgs | paperback: $17.95 | eBook: $9.99
Life would be so much easier if Lina were afraid of something
basic—like spiders—instead of something significant. Something like
real, true, healthy love.

Schuss – E. J. Noyes
978-1-64247-430-5 | 276 pgs | paperback: $17.95 | eBook: $9.99
They're best friends who both want something more, but what if
admitting it ruins the best friendship either of them have had?